IMPERFECTLY DELICIOUS

MARY FRAME

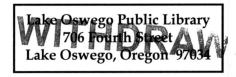

This book is dedicated to healthcare workers everywhere. Thank you for risking yourselves and your families to keep the world safe <3

Chapter One

IF ANYTHING IS GOOD FOR POUNDING HUMILITY INTO YOU permanently, it's the restaurant business.
  —Anthony Bourdain

Scarlett

FRED STEPS over me to reach the order window, an exaggerated motion that makes her dark ponytail swish behind her. "Confrontation is your kryptonite," she says over her shoulder.

"Do not tell him I'm here or you're fired." It's a threat that would carry more weight if I weren't a grown woman cowering on the floor of my own food truck in unequivocal terror.

She's not wrong. I like dealing with conflict as much as I enjoy public speaking while scorpions crawl all over my face.

It's not that I'm a total doormat. I deal with a variety of challenges and complications with ease. After all, I started my own food truck. I hired an employee—one who isn't very respectful or deferential, but who's counting? —and I run my own successful catering business as a side hustle.

I can totally adult. But talking to people who have a problem with me? Not my strongest suit.

And there is one person in particular who has *many* problems with me.

"Where is she?"

Guy Chapman.

His voice is as powerful as lightning in a summer storm—as if the air molecules themselves divided in terror at his words.

"She's hiding," Fred says.

I pinch her ankle and she kicks at me with the top of her foot, bumping into my side with more force than necessary. I scowl up at her but it's wasted effort, my glare striking the underside of her chin as she leans on the counter toward my nemesis.

This isn't the first time he's been here, and it's not the first time I've avoided him. We're parked in a narrow lot adjacent to his restaurant. I have the perfect view of his door when it swings open, an intricately carved, thick wood piece. It probably cost more than my life is worth.

He sighs like he can't believe he has to listen to such drivel, then says in a flat voice, "She's hiding. Why would she be hiding?"

"Because you're very scary," Fred stage whispers.

There's a small pause. "I am not." Is that a thread of dismay lacing his voice?

Can't be. He doesn't care if he's scary. That was basically the theme of his reality TV show, *Devil's Kitchen*. It was all about him being a handsome devil and behaving like one, too. It only lasted a season, despite its popularity.

"Yeah, I don't think so either," she murmurs, tapping her fingers on the counter. She's getting anxious, probably at the line of customers forming behind my sworn adversary.

Even though we're parked too close to the devil for comfort, there's no denying this is the best place I've found to park in the city. Situated on the south side of Gramercy Park, it's close enough to where the Wall Street gurus work to make it absolutely worthwhile for them to stop by when they're heading home and need something sweet along the way.

He owns the block, but not this tiny little slice. And much to my satisfaction, he never will.

"When will she be available?" he asks.

Fred thinks about an answer while I examine her shoes. There's a small hole in one seam at the top of her low-top black and white Vans, right next to a Ravenclaw patch.

"If I had to guess," she says finally. "I'd say never. She doesn't want to talk to you. I also can't tell her what to do, since she's my boss. You know how it is. I mean, you don't know how it is, but you have people who know how it is."

Laughter bubbles in my chest. But Guy Chapman isn't laughing. Oh no, I can't see him, but I can imagine the glower. His scowl can be felt within a three-mile radius.

I haven't seen him up close in over a year, but I have watched him from a distance over the past few weeks, coming and going to his restaurant while they get it up and running. Everything about him screams efficiency, from his neatly trimmed dark hair to his perfectly tailored business casual suits. His features are strong and severe: sharp nose, sculpted jawline—always impeccably shaved, facial hair wouldn't dare appear before five P.M.—and a thin slash of a mouth that would sooner crack into the earth than into a smile.

His features, on their own, are too much on the other side of harsh to be considered conventionally handsome. It's his confidence when he moves, the forcefulness of his speech, the way his presence demands attention and obedience—he exudes a force of character that is entirely overwhelming. He's like 125% of a person inside a body.

He's too much to handle. Which is why the last time I saw Guy Chapman up close, I may have accidentally set him on fire.

It's still silent up above. Is he leaving? Is he gone? It is over?

"Is this how you run a business?" His words are like the snap of a kitchen towel, quick and biting.

I cringe from my position crouched down low.

Fred, however, is not impressed. "It's not my business, and since the person in charge is trembling at my feet, I don't think she runs it well either, but you make an excellent point. I've got customers to serve and I don't think they're lining up for the smell of asshole in the afternoon, even if you were on a reality show three years ago. Do you mind stepping aside?"

Guy makes a disgusted noise, like he's unable to clear a particularly tough glob of phlegm from the back of his throat, and then he says, "If you see her, if she actually exists that is, please tell her I need to speak with her. Right away."

"I will for sure!" Fred's voice is bright and happy. "So, what was your name?"

Ominous silence.

This is the third time this week that Guy has come over here, and every time, Fred's asked him the same thing.

"Guy Chapman," he bites out.

"Right. Got it. I'll remember it this time." A few fraught seconds later, Fred starts taking an order for a dozen bite-size When Life Gives You Lemon cupcakes, and I peer carefully over the counter in the direction of Decadence.

Guy is stalking back to his restaurant, head high, the line of his shoulders rigid.

"You can't avoid him forever," Fred tells me while she rings up the customer.

"I can try." I stand up and move over to the counter on the opposite side where we've racked the cupcakes to help her box up the goods.

"You knew parking here would bring the troll from under the bridge."

I didn't know. And once I did, it didn't matter. There weren't any other good choices and failure wasn't an option. Besides, I didn't think he would even notice my little truck. We aren't doing anyone any harm.

"I can't believe you told him I was hiding from him."

She shrugs. "He didn't believe me. He's an idiot."

When I first parked here, I didn't know Guy was in the middle of renovations on the giant building next to this lot. And even if I had known, it wouldn't have deterred me. Finding decent parking for a food truck in New York City is like finding a tapdancing unicorn: both impossible and fantastic.

Fortunately for me, a friend owns this empty lot—her company does, anyway—and she offered to let me use it.

"I hadn't really expected it to affect his business at all," I tell Fred.

To be honest, I had both hoped and feared that parking my food truck outside Guy's newest restaurant venture would piss him off. Show him that his attempts to push me down hadn't worked. But I didn't expect to have to talk to him. I didn't expect him to lower himself to the point where he would come over and confront me directly.

Fred shrugs. "Clearly you've done something to get his attention if the King himself is deigning to mingle with the commoners."

We switch places and I plaster a smile on my face before greeting the next customer.

"Welcome to For Goodness Cakes, how can I help you?"

My body goes through the motions of ringing up orders and boxing up cupcakes for the after-work crowd, but my mind is still on the man who's disappeared inside his restaurant across the street.

It just plain doesn't make sense. I mean, he's Guy Chapman. He's a famous chef. He's been on TV. He's renowned for his culinary skills, business acumen, and sexy brooding demeanor. All of his restaurants are Michelin rated. He only hires the best—which knocked me out of the running before I could even start. The fire bit didn't help.

I didn't mean to torch him. Normally, I'm very meticulous and safe in the kitchen. It was just that he flustered me. He was standing so close, and he smelled like an expensive forest. Not like a normal woodsy pine scent, but like a fancy forest where the birds wear Rolexes and the deer drive Teslas. He was behind me, so close and leaning in and I…basically lost my mind.

I can't imagine that my business is affecting him enough for him to need to "speak" to me about anything. My proceeds are not even enough to live off of yet—although I'm creeping into the black. Catering is a necessity since winters in New York City can be harsh and customers won't likely shovel themselves out of their apartments or brave below-freezing temps.

Fred and I move around the narrow food truck, ringing up orders and switching places as needed. The timer sounds on the oven and Fred calls out, "I got it," before standing in front of it, holding up a hand and saying, "Live long and prosper." It's like her thing, since the oven is a Vulcan.

She insists it's good luck, and I can't complain because it makes me laugh. I don't know what I would do without Fred. She's a true New Yorker, born and raised. She's the only person I've ever met who can walk, talk, eat, and hail a cab all at the same time. She's super into fandoms and wears clothes that I don't understand 90%

of the time. She's ballsy and confrontational, but at the same time there's a hint of innocence and naivete about her, especially when it comes to her long-term boyfriend. She lets him run all over her. She's only a little bit older than my little sister, Reese. In a way I feel responsible for Fred.

I turn to the next customer. "Welcome to—oh it's you. Come to spy again?"

Before Guy started hounding the truck, he sent a lackey in his stead—Carson something or other. He's a tall, thin hipster who always wears bow ties and suspenders but somehow makes it cool and sleek instead of weird and passé. He always orders the specials.

The line has dissipated and he's the last one.

"I'm not spying," Carson says. "I like your cakes. Do you ever make hummingbird cake?"

"You know what that is?" Hummingbird cake is a true southern specialty: banana pineapple spice cake flavored with cinnamon, pecans, vanilla and a cream cheese frosting.

"Darling, despite the fashionable man you see before you, I hail originally from the backwoods of Moultrie, Georgia."

I gasp. "No! You don't even have an accent."

Personally, I've been working on talking more like a Yank so I don't come across as a hick. There is a more than a little bit of stereotyping when it comes right down to it.

He shrugs. "Can you make it?"

"I'm Southern and I bake. What do you think?"

Fred cuts in, handing him a container with the three

daily specials. "We'll make your weird cake if you give us some intel in return."

He taps one long finger on his bottom lip. "It might be worth it, actually. Despite what you think of my intentions, your product is excellent. Why else do you think Guy cares so much?"

"Cares?" Fred scoffs. "He only cares about himself."

"That's not true." He pops open the small pink box and his eyes brighten at the cakes.

Even though he's technically the enemy, I can't help but take delight in his reaction. It's the best part of my job. I love feeding people. Everyone is happy when there's cake.

"It is true," Fred insists. "I don't know how you work for that monster and live to talk about it, let alone defend him."

"He's not as bad as everyone thinks." He shoves one of the bites into his mouth and his eyes fall shut as he chews. "This one is definitely my new favorite," he tells me, frosting sticking out of the sides of his mouth.

Fred pushes a couple of napkins at him. "You're right, he's not as bad as everyone thinks, he's worse."

"Guy is a little bit of a perfectionist, but that's not a bad thing." Carson dabs at his mouth with the napkin.

I enter the conversation with a laugh. "Perfectionist is an understatement. If you're not a robot you'll likely get fired within a week. He's not only a perfectionist, he demands it from everyone around him."

Carson cocks his head at me. "How do you know?"

"She has ears and eyes," Fred says before I can reply, saving me from revealing the truth.

Technically, I've never actually worked for Guy. I only had an interview in one of his kitchens, but didn't make it past that process. Due to the whole, you know, fire incident.

"Why does he keep coming over here?" I ask.

Carson shrugs. "He wants you to move. He's got a plan for this area and you're in the way. It's not personal."

I'd figured as much, yet the audacity of the man still stings. "And he thinks, what, that he can snap his fingers and we'll do his bidding?"

"It generally works that way for him, yes."

"Well he can't boss me around."

"If you say so." He is clearly unconvinced.

Fred and I exchange a glance. The only reason I'm parking here is because my friend Bethany found the available real estate when she was going over Crawford and Company assets, and it's too small for them to use for anything at the moment, or to sell. They had originally owned the entire block, but then had sold off pieces over the years and this is all that's left. Bethany brokered me a killer deal to rent the space, an amount that's significantly less than what I would pay in parking tickets if I tried for anywhere else, but Guy could make this a problem. I can't ask them not to sell if he's going to make them an offer.

It's true that I have a few friends in high places—friends who own random real estate around Manhattan—but at the end of the day, I'm still an unknown hick with nothing to show for it but baking skills and a whole lotta motivation to make it in the big city and not go crawling back to Blue Falls with my tail tucked between my legs.

Carson picks up the Rhett Velvet and pops it in his mouth with a groan. "How do you make these so good?"

"It's a gift. Has he put in an offer for this lot?" I ask.

"We have someone working on it."

Fred makes a derisive noise.

"What? It's only a matter of time. Despite who you may know at Crawford and Company, money is louder than friendship."

Fred says, "We don't just know someone at Crawford and Company, we know one of the founders. As a matter of fact, the whole family is super tight with Scarlett, so you just try it, buddy."

Fred! I slap a hand over her mouth. Carson watches us, a half-smile on his face.

"It's been great talking to you Carson, but we have to prep for an event tonight."

"Do you?" He's intrigued. "Which event?"

"Not telling you. We've given you enough for one visit."

"Oh, come on."

"Bye, Carson." Fred closes the window on his surprised face and then turns to me. "Sorry. I get a little defensive and my mouth moves without my permission. But it'll be fine. I didn't give him much to go on. And you need to go home and get ready. I'll head to the commissary and get the stuff to the event within the hour."

"Thank you, Fred. You're a life saver." Literally. She does so much more than take orders on the truck and bake. She helps with social media, she does a lot of local deliveries, and she sometimes cleans and parks the truck at the commissary. Something we have to do every night, as required by the New York Health Department. Or as I like to call them, the people who bring on the pain and make things as difficult as humanly possible.

"Yeah, yeah." She waves me off. "Make sure you put on extra makeup before you go tonight because you look exhausted."

"Gee, thanks Fred. You sure you don't want to come with me?"

"Nah. I want to be home when Jack gets off work."

It must be nice to have someone to come home to. Once upon a time, I wanted it badly enough to date a whole variety of losers and users. It's not like I have high standards, I just have a vision in my head of what my life would be like—if I had someone. Someone to snuggle with on the couch while we argued over what to watch on TV. Someone I could call up for no real reason, just to have a mundane conversation about my day, or the weather, or how I got scared again by that guy who hides in the bushes by Mullaly Park. All of those ordinary moments made worthwhile simply by sharing them with someone who actually cares.

At least I have good friends and For Goodness Cakes. That has to be enough.

Chapter Two

CHEFS ARE NUTTERS. THEY'RE ALL SELF-OBSESSED, delicate, dainty, insecure little souls and absolute psychopaths. Every last one of them.

–Gordon Ramsay

Guy

I PUSH open the heavy wood door to Decadence and stalk through the empty dining area to the kitchen where about a half-dozen staff are laughing and talking.

One of them, the line cook, spots me at the door and his mouth slams shut. One by one, the rest of the group ceases conversation until only one employee is still laughing. After Julio nudges him with a shoulder, he turns and the laughter cuts off abruptly. He stands up straight, face pale, eyes on his feet. He's the newest hire. Julio's cousin. He vouched for him and now they're both downcast and subdued, as contrite as a couple of five-year-olds caught with their hands in the cookie jar.

"We've got one hour to prep. Get to work," I bark.

They immediately follow my bidding, feet scampering, dishes clanking faster and louder.

I head back to my office. Just outside the door, my assistant is sitting at his small desk, typing away at his laptop.

"Carson. Go find out something useful about that food truck."

"On it, boss." He gives me a jaunty salute and exits with almost too much haste.

Either he can't wait to get away from me, or those cupcakes are that good. The thought does nothing to ease my foul mood. Carson has been too willing to drop every-thing and rush over there.

I sit on the leather seat at the small desk and sort through the invoices Carson left in the tray on the corner, organized exactly the way I like it, by date and location. I check e-mails, responding to some marketing questions and forwarding requests for meetings to Carson for scheduling.

My alarm goes off at precisely five o'clock. I have to call the girls since I'll be home late, but first…

I pace out to the kitchen where the staff is busy and bustling, no more laughter and chatting. Quick and effi-cient movement, just like it should be.

I can control everything except the owner of that damn food truck. I can't even talk to her.

My phone dings with an incoming text. It's from one of my sisters—Emma, a series of random emojis. I send some back and then pick up the phone to call Clara and check on the girls.

Clara is a part-time nurse and caregiver. She helps me with my sisters' care and therapy and shuttles them to and from school when I can't. She's been a godsend—finding someone who can help watch over the girls and help Emma with various therapies was a true blessing.

While we're talking, Carson comes back in and sits at his desk outside my office and types furiously on his computer.

What is he doing?

Carson stands up and grabs something off our communal printer outside my office. Without making direct eye contact, he walks in and sits carefully in the chair opposite my desk, setting his notepad and printed materials in his lap, and waiting until I've finished my conversation.

"Well?" I ask after I've hung up with Clara.

"I found . . ." He sighs and meets my eyes. "I knew Scarlett had an inside connection with someone at Crawford and Company. But now I know who it is."

"Who?"

"Marc Crawford. His family are the original owners."

"How is that possible?" A two-bit chef, buddies with someone like that? Anyone can throw a small cake together and hack some frosting on it.

"About a year and half ago, there was an article." He sets papers in front of me. It's a printout of an article from the gossip website Page Seven. It's about Gwen McDougall, current fiancé to Marc Crawford. Marc's family owns Crawford and Company. I skim down the article, something about Gwen rescuing another woman from being drugged by a date.

"That's her." Carson points at a small, grainy, black and white photo of two women.

"Who? Gwen?"

"No, well, yes. The tall one is Gwen. The woman she's standing with? That's Scarlett Jackson."

I consider the poor-quality photo. Can't make out much more than a petite frame and small nose. The rest is a bit of a pixelated blur. Can't even tell the color of her eyes.

"So, you're saying she knows Marc's fiancé, but Marc doesn't even work there anymore." I rifle through the stack of new invoices set at the corner of my desk, searching for the ones from Crawford and Company. I'm sure I have the name of a rep somewhere…. I can hound someone about this, I'm sure of it.

Carson rolls his eyes. "It's a good thing you have me because you know nothing about anything important. Marc's still invested in the company. There's still some other connection, through Marc Crawford, and Scarlett has it."

I lean back in the seat and consider this new information. "That's how she got them to rent the space to her."

"Likely."

"And that's why they've been avoiding my calls to purchase. Oliver is not going to be pleased."

Carson taps a finger on his lips. "Maybe don't tell him?"

"Trust me, I'll keep it from him as long as I can, but I'm surprised he doesn't already know. The man has his fingers in everything. We'll get them to sell eventually, just not as cheaply as I had hoped. Maybe I can convince them otherwise. We're catering an event for one of Crawford's charities tonight." And I purchase all my kitchen equipment from them, have for years. They wouldn't want to lose me as a customer. I have to have some way to get them to see reason. Money matters more than friendship. I'm not worried. Much. Oliver would probably have some backhanded way of getting it done, but I want to prove my worth as his partner in this venture. He has too much power and control over this whole thing as it is, and it makes me uneasy.

Carson shrugs, his mustache twitching.

"Any other ideas on how to get her to move?"

He opens his laptop. "Oh, I don't know. Scare her into acquiescence like you do everyone else."

I press my lips together. "You make me laugh."

Carson shakes his head at me. "Right. All those times we've laughed together. It's weird." He rubs his chin. "It's like it happens so often that I can't even remember it."

I wave him off. "I'm laughing on the inside. Anyway, I would try to scare her into doing my bidding if I could actually see her. Every time I go over, she's not there. Her assistant actually told me she was hiding the last two times."

"Can you blame her? I'd avoid you too if you didn't know where I live and didn't pay me so well to put up with you."

I ignore his trash talking. "She's hard to catch. She has a visual advantage. She can see me coming and I can't see inside her truck. I don't have time to stalk her when she comes and goes. Maybe if I could run into her somewhere else, though, when she doesn't expect it."

Carson nods. "I've been doing some digging. I've got an idea, but you might not like it."

I sigh. I hate having to expend this energy on something that should have been resolved a month ago. Why did she have to park that monstrosity right next to my restaurant? "What is it?"

"She routinely goes to a yoga class. Every Thursday at six, in Manhattan. Lower East Side."

"Fine." I've done yoga. I can handle it if it means I can confront the cake lady. "Put all the information in my calendar and I'll be there."

A grin spreads across his face. He's almost too happy, and I want to know why, but I don't want to get roped into some inane conversation either. No time.

The office phone rings.

Carson whips around, darting back to his desk to answer it. Three seconds later, he calls out, "I've got Oliver."

I pick up the phone. "Oliver."

"Guy. Are we any closer to opening Savor?"

Straight to the point, as usual. Oliver isn't one for small talk.

"You know, even I can't change the laws of physics or movement of paper through the New York City Department of Consumer Affairs."

Oliver expels a breath of frustration down the line, the tension in the sound practically scalding my ear. "Why not? Do you need more money?"

I take a moment to gather my thoughts and roiling

emotions. I'd really thought I could handle Oliver. This venture, on the surface, was practically a dream come to life. Complete creative control, more time with my sisters, and monetary backing from a silent partner to see it all off the ground. Except my partner can't handle the whole part where I have any kind of control, likes to remind me of my obligation to him, and in general is not as silent as I had hoped.

"It's not about the money. It's just a matter of time," I say.

"You know how I feel about waiting. All of these setbacks are a bad sign. I agreed to do this because you told me it could be finished before the holidays."

"I said it was possible, not inevitable. The delay won't be more than a week or two. And we've already opened Decadence. We're booked out solid for months. The delay is working to our advantage, giving us time to build buzz and make the whole idea even more appealing."

There's a deep pause. The original idea was mine. A whole block dedicated to haute cuisine, in the nouvelle style, using the freshest ingredients, with simple prep to create lighter and more delicate flavors. Two restaurants, both menus controlled by me with guest chefs making appearances on a monthly basis to keep the ideas fresh and unique.

"What about the outdoor area?" he asks.

My hand clenches around the pen in my hand. It's all part of the original plan to utilize the entire block and provide a whole sensory experience to go along with the food. There will be twinkling lights, fountains, high-end heat lamps that blend into the greenery, fire pits, and comfortable outdoor seating.

"I'm working on it." If I could get my hands on a slippery food truck owner named…what was it? I pick up the article on the desk in front of me. Scarlett Jackson. For some reason, the name gives me a sense of déjà vu. Have I heard it before?

"Work faster, would you? This is a bad sign. I should have hired a different chef," he mumbles. And then he hangs up.

A pulse pounds in my head. He didn't *hire* me. We agreed on this deal together. I know better than to take it personally, this is just how he is. Damn Oliver and his crazy, eccentric, superstitious money. I need him to pull this off. I hate that I need him. I hate that he can cut out of this deal at any moment and won't lose a wink of sleep. I thought I could deal with him.

He's not entirely a dick, even though he's good at acting like one. I've known him since we were in high school. I was one of his only friends since most people thought he was a weirdo. He is, in fact, a brilliant weirdo who went from a poverty-stricken upbringing to billionaire with nothing more than his own hard work and razor-sharp mind. He's also one of the few people I know who enjoys hanging out with my sisters. They love him. So, I love him too, even when I want to strangle him. Which is why I agreed to this deal, with nothing in writing. I should have made him sign a contract agreeing to not be a total pain in my ass, but I might as well have asked for the Earth to stop rotating.

I was too excited at the possibility of being able to keep my career without it affecting raising my sisters.

I shove thoughts of Oliver and the food truck issue to the side and try to keep them there.

"Carson!"

He comes running back to his chair.

"Moving on," I snap. "Have we filed the paperwork for Marie?"

"Three more weeks. Almost four."

The other thorn in my side. You can't file for divorce based on abandonment until a year has passed. So close.

"Any word from John?" My attorney. The one helping me try to get a divorce.

Carson winces. "We still haven't been able to serve her papers."

This doesn't surprise me. We've been trying to get her for the past year, but Instagram is the only way to figure out where she is and she doesn't stay in one location long enough to pin her down and serve her papers. It's costing me an arm and a leg to get her served overseas, and she's been everywhere from the Maldives to Ibiza, hence my having to wait forever to file under the terms of abandonment.

"We're booked out for the next two months?"

He nods, his eyes brightening. "The exclusivity idea was brilliant. We could probably schedule out this way for years just because people want what they can't have."

Part of my deal with Oliver was being able to spend more time with my family. Which is why, for now, Decadence is only serving dinner and only by reservation for a few hours a night. We charge an exorbitant amount for the opportunity.

A muscle twitches in my eye as Carson rattles off a list of the details that are on fire over the next week—so much to do to make everything run smoothly. But it has to be perfect. Everything I need, and the girls need, is riding on this. Sometimes managing all this is like building a skyscraper out of the thinnest of wafers. One inadvertent sneeze could topple the entire thing.

"Guy?" Carson stares at me, head tilted in concern.

It probably wasn't the first time he said my name.

"What?"

He purses his lips. "As I was saying, for the charity event tonight, your tux is hanging in the bathroom, and the car is picking you up in an hour."

"Right." I sit up straighter and grab my pen from its place at the corner of my desk.

Carson continues, "The guys are already onsite, prepping for dinner."

"Got it." I click my pen. "Yes. Are we done here?"

"I guess, Cinderella." He stands up on a sigh, stopping at the doorway. "Have fun at the ball, be home by midnight lest you turn into a pumpkin."

Right. Because my life is such a fairy tale.

Chapter Three

THERE IS NO SINCERER LOVE THAN THE LOVE OF FOOD.
   –George Bernard Shaw

Scarlett

ONE OF THE best parts of living in the city is taking the subway. Sure, I've seen a rat or two, and sometimes the ride is boring and uneventful—or delayed—but every now and then you get a random person dressed as Pikachu in your car. Except he's sitting and taking up multiple seats so now I'm pole dancing next to a well-dressed businessman on one side and a very tall, very beautiful drag queen in red, who smiles and tells me I have a great dress, on the other.

I smile in thanks, the phone pressed to my ear preventing me from returning the compliment. The confidence boost is well timed as Granny screeches in my ear. "You're going to one of those fancy city parties?" Every time I'm on the phone with Granny she yells because she doesn't trust the technology to hear her. Also, I think she's losing her hearing but is too proud to admit it.

"Yes, Granny." I glance down at my outfit, a dark blue 1950s style sheath dress with kitten heels. "I'm wearing the lucky brooch you gave me." I even took the time to put on lipstick. I haven't worn this dress in a year. My normal uniform is a t-shirt and comfortable pants with a dirty apron.

"That brooch was the reason I married your grandpa; God rest his soul."

"It was?" I don't think I've heard this story. She always told me it belonged to her great Aunt Winifred and that Aunt Winnie was a black widow who murdered four of her five husbands.

"Yep. Aunt Winnie gave it to me because a voodoo priestess gave it to her to help her find love. That was right before her fifth husband."

"The one that she didn't murder?"

"That's right. It's a lucky brooch."

"If you say so," I murmur. Once upon a time, her words might have triggered a rush of hope, but not anymore. I've given up on love because it gave up on me a long time ago. Now I have cakes. And ten more pounds on my hips.

"What?" She shrieks and I pull the phone away from my ear a few inches.

"I said, if you say so," I repeat loudly.

She's silent for a second and then, "You sure you're okay to go out tonight? You sound as tired as a sex worker on dime night."

I snort out a laugh and the businessman shoots me a disgruntled glare and leans away.

"I'm only going for a little bit. It's for charity."

"Well, that's alright then, I suppose. You deserve to have a good time. At least you aren't working, I guess."

I hold my tongue and don't tell her about the order I'll have to make when I get home later tonight. It won't be my first late night baking session and I'm sure it won't be the last. Sometimes if it's a big one, Fred helps, but tonight I'm handling it myself. Most days I'm up at four o'clock in the morning, baking for the truck anyway.

"Tell me what's going on with Reese." I change the subject to something other than myself. "I can't believe she's living with two men. Do our parents know?" Not that they would care, but it feels like the right thing to say. Reese is only nineteen; while she's legally an adult, she's very naïve in a lot of ways and it worries me. It's her second year in college and she's never been a real social person, but she's finally made some friends and even has a boyfriend, just out of nowhere.

Despite my relief that she's making friends, I can't help but worry. I had been encouraging her to put herself out there, and now I'm not there to ensure she's making the right decisions. She is technically an adult though, so I have to trust that she knows what she's doing or she'll learn it herself.

"Your parents don't know nothin'. But I've got it all

handled. Don't you worry, Scarlett. They're good boys. They come over all the time to help me with my chorin'."

What she really means is they help her with her moonshine. This isn't making me feel better.

Who's the worse influence? Granny or some college kids? It's hard to say.

I still can't believe Reese has an actual boyfriend—who is not one of the men she's living with, apparently, thank heavens for that. It's just that…everyone has someone, except me. I shove that thought far, far away and tug at the neckline of my dress.

"I can hear your fussin' from here, Scarlett, and I'm gonna tell you it's all okay. If you are so vexed, you can come on down and see for yourself."

I bite my lip. "I'll be down for a little bit at Christmas." I managed to get a cheap seat on Christmas day. All my money has been sunk into the truck, and there's hardly anything left.

"You know, your parents will be in the city there for an art show or something in a couple weeks. You should go."

This is news. "They'll be in New York?"

"Yep."

"You're sure?" I ask.

It shouldn't sting that I'm just now hearing of this. I should be used to being ignored, but the surprise still hurts. They can't be bothered to call? Not even their assistant could let me know?

"I got it written down here, they'll be at the Harlem Underground. That's in Harlem."

"Got it, Granny. Are you sure they want me there?"

Why do I even bother asking when I know that they don't?

"If they don't then they're damn fools. You know how they are. Your father is like your grandpa, God rest his soul, but he couldn't find his own ass with two hands and a map."

I smile. She's not wrong. I didn't know my grandpa much, but my parents....

They were always so absorbed with their art and with each other that they often forgot Reese and I existed. The abandonment from my parents led me into chasing love and affection like a hound after rabbits. And then instead of being fuzzy and cuddly, they were vicious mammals out for blood.

The train comes to a stop.

"I gotta run, Granny. Love you. Give my love to Reese. Tell her I'll call her this weekend."

"You got it my girl, have extra fun tonight. Get into trouble, or something. I think you're due."

"It's only a charity dinner." I step off the train and into the station, moving around people and glancing around the space for the exit.

"It's like I always say, my dear, life is like beer and Skittles. Sometimes it's sweet, and sometimes it smells a little funky but it can still give you a buzz."

I laugh. Granny is always tossing out random expressions that don't make a lick of sense. A pang of homesickness slices through my chest. "Love you."

"DAMN, HOTTIE!" Bethany squeals in my ear, her arms draping over me in a hug. "Can we be sister wives?"

I laugh. "Of course. I'll break the bad news to Brent, later. This venue is amazing." I glance around the space, my eyes trailing over the high ceilings, glowing chandeliers, and formally dressed attendees. Even the servers are wearing tuxedos, weaving through the crowd carrying trays of hors d'oeuvres.

The event is being held at The Pierre, a way fancy hotel on 5th Avenue overlooking Central Park. It's like being in a movie. The walls are covered in intricate designs and wainscoting, lined with sconces placed strategically to add to the ambience of the space, the floors are sleek and shiny, and the tables have all been decorated with elegant white bouquet centerpieces.

She carefully extricates herself from around me; one of my mini cupcakes is in her hand and the frosting passes right before my eyes, almost scraping my nose.

"Thank you so much for bringing the cupcakes," she says, holding it up. "The kids love them, but not as much as I do. I had to fight off three of them for this one." She motions over to a table where a few of the kids are stuffing their faces, along with some adults. The kids are so cute in their little suits.

"Cake makes everyone happy," I say.

"No joke. Come on, our table is over here near the front."

"You did an amazing job with this event," I tell her.

She waves it off. "I have a thousand people working for me. I just get to tell them what to do."

Bethany moved to New York late last year and took over the lease on Gwen's apartment while Gwen was traipsing all over the world taking pictures. She got a job at Crawford and Company as assistant to the CEO—Mr. Crawford himself—but took over a managerial position when he retired.

She grabs my arm and we move through the crowd but it's slow going because we're stopped every couple of feet. Bethany introduces me to each person, most of whom are employees from Crawford and Company. Some are football players that must have come because of Bethany's man, Brent Crawford. He was the tight end of the New York Sharks until a medical condition took him off the field last year.

"Make sure you check out the art show outside, there are some interactive walk-in exhibits and a silent auction!" Bethany calls back to some quarterback as we meander our way through clusters of people.

"Walk-in art exhibit? I'll have to check it out."

"It's interesting," Bethany says.

I smile at her, but then over her shoulder, a familiar figure in the crowd makes me do a double take.

"Bethany." I grip her arm.

She looks down at my hand squeezing her bicep. "Is there a good reason you're going all anaconda on me right now?"

"Why is Guy Chapman here?"

She follows my gaze and then nods. "Oh, yeah, him? One of his places did the dinner service. Why do you think we were able to charge $500 a plate? He's like a big deal or whatever. Do you know him?"

"You could say that." My stomach clenches. I can't seem to get away from him. What if he sees me?

Her eyes brighten. "Let's go talk to him."

"No!"

Her brows lift at my sudden vehemence and then she grins. "There's a story here and I have to know it. Tell me everything."

"I can't. I can't be around him. I lose all control and then bad things happen."

Her eyes widen and I immediately regret the mouth slip. Bethany is stubborn and determined and will torture the truth out of me. "I'm intrigued." Her arm tightens on mine. "What happened?"

"Nothing important. I mean, I have to pee. Be right back."

I push at her to unlock my arm from her death grip and do what I'm good at—run away.

"You're such a liar!" she calls after me. "I know where you live, Scarlett!"

I keep going, too chicken to turn around and see if Guy heard her or noticed my abrupt departure and the subsequent yelling.

Maybe he didn't. Maybe he won't make the connection; I'm sure there's more than one Scarlett in New York City. Unless he's noticed the cupcakes…. Gosh darn it, my business cards are all over that table. If he sees me, I'm sunk.

I need to hide until dinner. By then everyone will be sitting and he won't catch sight of me and I'll survive another day. Dramatic, much? Maybe.

I escape out the first side door I come across. It opens

into a wide hallway with cream walls speckled with prints and photographs of various sizes. Free standing sculptures dot the open space.

There's a table set up to the side with silent auction boxes. A few people linger at the tables, filling out their bid sheets.

"We'll be starting the speeches in twenty minutes," the attendant by the door tells me. "At which time we won't be allowing people back in to avoid interruptions."

"Right. Got it. Thank you." I smile.

There are about a dozen people walking around inspecting the pieces. It's a lot quieter and less crowded than the ballroom.

I take a few deep breaths and wander through the hall, stopping to inspect some of the artwork. Some of them are Gwen's photographs from her travels. Seeing them makes me miss her. I wish she could be here. I gaze at one of her pieces of a young child draped in colorful beads smiling at the camera, eyes gleaming with excitement. There's another photograph of woven baskets. Then next to that, an amazing shot of a group of people dancing, their robes swirling and the colors making it appear almost like they're in motion.

Down a side hall, I find the walk-in installation Bethany was talking about, literally a giant black box with an open doorway.

It's like a free-standing room, ten by ten and at least seven feet tall. The outside is painted midnight black, but the entrance is curved, and the interior walls are bright white and sparkling with a swirly pattern.

I make my way inside. The open top provides the only

illumination. The free-standing room is split into two sections by a low set wall. Set on top of the waist high divider are viewfinders. Behind the barrier is an empty, open space covered in the same swirled texture of the rest of the walls, a concave gap of sparkly curves. I approach the closest viewing box and bend over to peek inside.

There's a button to push that turns on a light bulb. I push it, half expecting something deep and poetic, but it's a hot dog. With only mustard. Who eats hot dogs like that? And why is there a hot dog at all?

The next viewfinder has a big toe made of some kind of Play-Doh material.

That's weird. And a little creepy.

I pull away to move onto the next one, but my progress is halted by a tug on my dress. It's my brooch, must be caught on the wall material. I give it a tug but it's stuck good to one of the swirly patterns that's giving the walls that shiny appearance. I feel carefully around the brooch where it's latched, not wanting to rip my dress.

The pretty swirly pattern is jagged and pointed and sharper than it appears. The filigree on my brooch is caught around a sharp edge. I tug harder, twisting in one direction and then the other.

It's still stuck.

Sweat beads on the back of my neck. I can't get up. I'm stuck here, bent over and awkward. I really hope no one walks in, but at the same time, I'm not sure I can escape this on my own.

With a burst of panic, I give it a hard yank and turn and my brooch breaks free—from the wall and my dress —and goes flying up, shimmering mid-air in front of me for a brief second before plummeting to the floor on the other side of the short partition wall.

I let out a breath, thankful to be free, except…I finger the bodice of my dress, locating a tear. But maybe I can retrieve my brooch and use it to cover up the dress. Pull it together at any rate.

I lean, stretching over the squat partition. Of course, it fell against the opposite wall, as far away as possible. I reach for it in the low light, but I'm too short.

Stretching further, I fumble, feet leaving the ground.

Finally, finally, my fingers wrap around the brooch and I slide back only to yelp when I get halted again. This time, it's my hair.

Oh no. My fancy up-do is caught on something. I think it's the opposite wall.

I reach my free hand up to figure out where my hair got caught. Carefully, I try to extricate the strands, pulling back every few seconds to check if the grip has loosened, but the pressure doesn't change, and I can't tell if I'm making it better or worse.

Hesitantly, I attempt to lean back further and am immediately caught up. Now even a slight tug hurts.

Worse. I've made it worse.

"Now I'm really in a pickle," I mutter to myself. I don't know whether to laugh or cry.

"I'm not sure that's the proper way to view this particular piece of art," a masculine voice says behind me.

Mortification threads its way through the relief pounding inside me. "I'm afraid I've got myself a little stuck . . ." With one hand, I wave in the direction of my head.

My rescuer moves to my side. I can't see much of him —my vision is blocked by red tendrils that loosened in my struggles—but I can see he's wearing a tux. Gentle fingers tug at my hair.

"How did you even manage this?" The voice is rough and deep but flavored with a hint of humor, and additional heat fills my already hot face.

"I have a knack for finding myself in strange and embarrassing situations. It's a real gift."

His hands still for a moment. "Stranger than getting your hair caught in an interactive art exhibit?"

"Oh, yes. One time, in high school, my shirt got stuck in Jeffrey Potter's braces, in the middle of a school play. Oh, and there was the time after one of my first job interviews. I got up, shook everyone's hand and then walked into a coat closet."

He leans over me a bit more, his chest pressing into my shoulder and shaking with what I think is laughter, but I don't hear any chuckles coming from his mouth. Odd.

"How did your shirt get caught in someone's braces? I've almost got you out now," he says. The rumble of his chest against my shoulder sends a strange tingle through me but that might be the blood rushing to my head. Also, I haven't been this close to a man in way too long and he smells way too good. And familiar, somehow.

"It was a combination of too much flailing with a loose shirt and Jeffrey Potter being a mouth breather." I focus on his wrists and fingers. They're nice. Strong and sensitive. He has small scars on the one thumb I can focus on. Before I can ogle his hands anymore, a final tug frees my hair and I stand up and turn to thank my rescuer.

All the heat in my face rushes from my head to my feet and—oh, no.

My kind and thoughtful rescuer is *him*.

Guy Chapman.

Panic slides through me like water through a sieve.

He's found me. I try to swallow past the lump in my throat and promptly start coughing and choking on my own spit.

He claps me on the back. "Are you okay?"

I struggle to retain control and get the liquid out of my windpipe without coughing spittle in his face but the area is confined and there are not many ways I can turn.

Heat suffuses my neck and face. I'm a human heat lamp and my eyes are a messy watering pot.

Oh God, I'm going to die here next to my sworn enemy and all the paramedics will see my runny mascara face and mottled complexion. And I'm wearing my laundry panties.

His presence hovers next to me like a specter or other menace, like maybe a demon. He's going to do something to speed my death along, I'm sure of it. That way I won't be parking my pathetic truck near his fancy restaurant.

But he doesn't try to kill me. He doesn't harass me about my truck.

Instead he continues to pat me on the back gently and asks again, "You alright?"

Not exactly a demonic phrase, in and of itself.

I nod, wiping my eyes with a finger to avoid smudging my mascara too roughly, and clear my throat a couple of times for good measure. "Fine, fine. Just, uh, swallowed wrong."

I keep my gaze focused down, surreptitiously cleaning up my face and avoiding direct contact.

My heart thumps a dull beat in my chest. My body is tensed for fight or flight.

After a few quiet seconds that last a lifetime, I can't help but peek.

I lift my chin, tense but determined. I'm not doing anything wrong. I will fight him. Or grovel and beg for mercy. One of those.

Our eyes meet, mine likely wide and terrified in my skull.

Hazily, I recognize the brightness of his gaze. It's been so long since we've been this close, I had forgotten about his eyes. They're green—not a normal, hazel green but a bright, vibrant, impossible green. Blade of grass green that is generally accompanied by an intimidating glare. But he's not scowling like I expected. His gaze is steady, but tired. Worn around the edges like an old pair of gloves. The rest of him is as put together as ever, except for the slight scruff on his jaw.

I expect his expression to phase into something unpleasant once he realizes who I am, but it doesn't happen.

There's no flicker of recognition. No shocked gasp. No, "It's you! Evil spawn of Satan cupcake confectioner!"

Just the weary gaze and very slight upward twist to his lips.

In a burst of shock, the truth showers over me like expired rainbow sprinkles.

He doesn't know who I am. How is this possible?

It's true that he hasn't actually seen me in a year—at

least not up close—as a result of my excellent ninja skills. But still.

How do you forget someone who set you on fire? I mean, literally. I set him on fire. Was it that forgettable?

What the heckerino do I do now?

Chapter Four

Guy

WHO IS THIS WOMAN?

There's something about her that's vaguely familiar. But I'm sure I would remember those deep blue eyes—the color only heightened by her pinkened cheeks—and her hair. Long, with a slight curl. And that color — a deep red that matches her eyebrows.

"Who are—?" I start.

"Uh, is someone in there?" A voice calls out from the entrance.

I twist around. There's a man in a suit standing in the

curved entrance, mostly blocking a row of children behind him who are laughing and chattering and waiting their turn to come into the exhibit.

They must have heard the grunting and panting and coughing. "Just a minute, please. We've had uh, a little situation." I spin back to the redhead.

Her fathomless blue eyes widen, and she tries to fumble her hair back into place while simultaneously pulling up at her top. "Stop that. You make it sound like we've been fornicating," she whispers loudly.

Her choice of words makes my lips tickle and I press them together. "Fornicating?" I say in a normal volume.

"Shhhh!" She flaps one hand in my direction while her other hand fumbles at her dress where she's attempting to pin a brooch over a giant tear in the fabric.

"Uh, we can hear you." The man outside says. "There are kids out here, this isn't the place or time for this kind of behavior."

"We're almost done," I call out, and then lower my voice. "Can I help you?"

She glares at me, lips tightening. "No, you cannot help me cover my bosom."

"That's not what I meant. I can fix," I wave a hand at her head, "your hair."

Did she really say bosom?

Her mouth twists with suspicion. "You can?"

"I have experience with women's hair."

Her lips press into a thin line and a small crease appears between her brows.

I don't mention I watched a ton of YouTube tutorials

and learned how to do a variety of styles at the behest of two rambunctious teen girls.

"They're not naked," a small voice declares. A little kid in a suit peeks around the corner. I catch a glimpse of overly gelled hair, but still not enough to prevent a few cowlicks, along with raised brows and a clip-on tie. "She looks like she got attacked by a bear! Was it a polar bear?"

"No bears in here," I call out, then I lift a brow at her hesitation. "You're welcome to take care of it yourself or we can . . ." I gesture toward the only exit.

Her expression can only be described as mutinous. And about as effective as an angry puppy.

"Turn around." I motion with a hand.

She takes a deep breath but then turns, posture rigid. "What are you going to do?"

"I was thinking about a mohawk. Sound good?"

"What?" Her voice rises a few octaves, shoulders rising with tension.

"Relax. I know what I'm doing."

She grumbles but must be aware that she doesn't have much of a choice unless she wants to rejoin the party looking like a flame-haired, ravaged Medusa.

There are a few bobby pins sticking out in varying directions. I gently release the strands from their clutches and then thread my fingers into the silky gloss of her hair. She smells like vanilla and sugar.

My stomach tightens.

Maybe this was a bad idea.

I attempt to ignore the thoughts and images flickering through my head of this same hair spread over a pillow.

Down, boy.

"Is it our turn yet?" A child yells from outside.

"Almost," I call back.

Once I can focus, it takes less than a couple of minutes for me to deftly weave her hair into a braid. And still, I can't help but notice as my ministrations expose the gentle curve of her neck as it winds into her shoulder, a perfect slope of soft skin.

"There. Now you're all put together and there is no evidence of fornicating."

She faces me, a hand fluttering over the back of her head. "Did you…braid my hair?"

"Yes. Don't get excited, it's only a French braid. No time for something more intricate like a fishtail."

She frowns. "How do you—?"

"Are you guys done in there yet?"

Her face is beet red, but we exit and I nod at the other patrons and gently steer her down the hall while she covers up the front of her dress.

"Thank you for your assistance. I have to…find the bathroom." She motions to where she's holding together her clothes.

I point down the hall. "It's down there, to the right."

"Right. Thanks for all your help. I can take it from here. Maybe." She gives an awkward wave and grimace before walking speedily to the bathroom.

As she disappears, a strange sort of fascination twists through me. I'm not sure what to make of her. All I know is I want to hear her say more things, like fornication and bosom and getting her clothes caught in someone's braces. Maybe I should wait here, make sure she's okay. What if she can't fix her dress and she needs . . . something? My tux jacket. That would cover her, and then some.

I wait for a few minutes, but then a few minutes turns into ten. I wonder if I should ask her if she needs help— what if she got herself in another situation, stuck to the sink or something? —but second-guess myself. What am I doing anyway, stalking someone outside the bathroom? She's going to think I'm a creep. I *am* being a creep. Shaking my head, I walk back in the direction of the ball-room but when I arrive, the doors are shut and there's an attendant standing sentry.

She gives me an apologetic smile. "Sorry. The speeches have started so we aren't letting anyone in for another thirty minutes."

"No problem." I step off to the side and stop in front of a charcoal print of an old man, gazing at it blankly.

A short time later, the attendant speaks again. "Sorry, speeches have started. We still have about twenty-five minutes until we can let people back in."

"Oh. Right."

I turn at the voice, recognizing the low cadence.

She's fixed her dress. Sort of. She's stuffed some paper towels into her top. I bite my lip so the smile doesn't break free.

She faces me.

"I know, it's terrible," she says before I can make any comments. "I'm probably just going to leave." She's flustered, her eyes touching every object in the general vicinity except for me.

It makes me crave her focus even more.

"It's not…too bad." I grimace.

Now her dark blue gaze sweeps to mine and her lip tilts up on one side. "You're a terrible liar."

I shrug. "Lying has always seemed pointless."

"I suppose so." She crosses her arms over her chest, but it doesn't completely cover the paper towel sticking up out of the top of her dress.

"When is it ever a good idea to lie?" I ask, mostly just wanting to keep the conversation going. Wanting to hear her talk. There's a lilt in her voice, and I'm trying to place it.

Her nose wrinkles. "When you don't want to hurt someone's feelings, maybe?"

"But if they ultimately discover the truth anyway, wouldn't that be worse?"

"Probably."

She fidgets with her dress, twitching next to me and clearly uncomfortable.

"Would you like to wear my jacket?"

She immediately shakes her head. "No, thanks."

"You're sure?"

"Well." She glances back at the attendant who's studiously avoiding watching us. "Maybe."

I shrug it off and hand it to her.

"Thanks. I'll make sure you get this back before I leave."

She pulls it on, the fabric dwarfing her small frame and an odd sense of proprietary gratification sweeps through me.

What is that?

It's nothing. I clear my throat and glance around, looking for something else to focus on. "No problem.

What do you think about this print?" I nod to the charcoal drawing of an old man. It's all dark colors and rough smudges, highlighting his wrinkles and prominent features. His face is worn and sad.

"He has kind eyes," she says.

I study her profile in surprise and then turn back to the piece. "I guess you're right." I didn't notice that bit.

"I bet he's the type of grandpa that tells poop jokes to his grandkids, and he's retired from some important job like mayor or neurosurgeon. He probably goes to the same coffee shop every morning and they know him by name, but he hardly ever speaks. When he does, it's to impart something profound. Like, 'What we think, we become'."

I stare at the portrait and then back at her. "You got all that from this?"

Her smile is brighter than the sconce on the wall. "Didn't you?"

I step over to the side. "What about this one?"

We walk around the gallery and she makes up stories about each portrait and I don't think I've ever been so entertained, or as intrigued, by anyone in my life—even though she's jumpy. Even with my jacket on, she fidgets with her dress and is careful to maintain distance between us. A distance that starts to bother me, even though I can't quite put my finger on why.

"Your boyfriend must be a happy man," I say at one point. Yes, I'm digging, but I can't help it.

The comment must surprise her, because she stumbles and nearly runs into a sculpture.

I reach out and clasp her elbow with gentle fingers.

"Careful." Once she's stable, I still don't let go. I don't want to.

"I don't have a boyfriend," she says. She doesn't step back like I expect since she's been so skittish around me. We're standing only a foot apart. The narrow hallway is empty.

Her tongue slips out and wets her bottom lip and it's like a tractor beam. Magnetic force. She's staring at my mouth, and her pupils are dilated, and her breathing starts to quicken, setting up an answering pulse in my chest.

"I just want you to be aware," her voice isn't much more than a whisper, "that this is all your fault." She leans in and presses her mouth against mine.

Shock sweeps through me, but sliding along the instant after is a soothing wave of rightness. Like up until this moment, my body was a jumble of random ingredients that have now miraculously settled into the perfect three-course meal.

Her lips are sweeter than spun sugar and with one simple touch, everything inside me ignites in a blaze of desire. It makes no sense. Where did this come from? This isn't like me. I don't do this. Not with random women at charity events or anywhere else.

Thoughts fly away when her tongue slips between my lips and she makes a pleasurable little noise in the back of her throat. I slide a hand down her back, gripping her ass and pulling her harder against me.

Her hands are greedy and fumbling. She untucks my shirt from my pants and her fingers play up my back, inciting a wave of tingles and goosebumps in their wake. Maybe it's because I've been without adult companionship for so long, but something about this moment strikes me as significant. Her mouth is both a comforting caress and a brutal ache of insistent longing that needs fulfillment.

Children's laughter fills the air as the door to the event slams open and she goes stiff in my arms. She wrenches away, her hands disappearing from my skin. With a whispered word that could have been goodbye, but is really more of an awkward mumble, she disappears.

I would stop her if a swarm of elementary aged children didn't choose that moment to crowd the hallway between us, and if I wasn't in a complete haze of lust and confusion about what the hell just happened—my heart still pounding out of my chest. When I finally come back to myself, I'm standing in the hall still surrounded by kids, dazed and bewildered.

My phone beeps and I glance at the time. I was supposed to check on the kitchen staff before dinner service. Which is happening right now.

I'm late.

I'm never late.

I take a deep breath to compose myself and haul ass to the kitchen. The staff is startled by my sudden appearance, but thankfully they're trained well enough that after a few barked orders and strange glances sent my way, they get back to plating the first course to my exacting specifications.

Once it's ready to be brought out to the banquet hall, I let the sous chef take over; I take a moment to gather my mind, washing my hands in the giant kitchen sink.

There's a stainless-steel paper towel dispenser next to

the sink, and I reach for it, catching my reflection in the mirrored surface. I have red lipstick all over my mouth.

I press my lips together and wipe it off with a towel. I have to find her. I head out into the event, walking the perimeter, eyeing tables, searching for a flash of red hair, or blue dress.

But she's gone.

Poof. Like an apparition that slipped through my fingers

No real goodbye. No "Can I get your number?"

I don't even know her name.

I spot Bethany Connell, the woman from Crawford and Company who hired me. She's over at a table to the side, sorting through a box of papers.

"Hey." I stop next to her, getting her attention. "Have you seen a woman with red hair?"

"Who?" She frowns down at the papers—the silent auction bid sheets.

"There was a woman here, earlier, she had red hair. She was wearing a blue dress. Do you know who she is? Or where she went?"

Her eyes scan me, a slight frown on her face. "Oh, yes. I do and yes, she left."

"What's her name?"

She eyes me again, her head tilting to one side. "That's, uh, Mildred."

"Mildred?"

"Yep. Don't know her last name, sorry. I gotta go set up the stuff for the auction items." She smiles, the movement forced, and then she pats me on the shoulder perfunctorily and disappears into the crowd.

My lips twist. She didn't look like a Mildred, not that there's anything wrong with having a name like a grandmother from the 1920s, but...

Like Cinderella, she's fled the ball and I have no clue who she really is. And she has my tux jacket.

Chapter Five

KNOWLEDGE IS THE FOOD OF THE SOUL.
  —Plato

Guy

"WHAT DOES THIS WOMAN LOOK LIKE?" I ask Carson, pressing the phone to my ear to hear him over the buzz of traffic as I navigate a busy intersection.

Always keep your eye out for the Yellow Cab: one of the first rules of living in the city.

It's Thursday. Yoga day. Time to finally have a discussion with the food truck woman.

"She's petite," Carson says. "Red hair. Like deep red, unusual. You can't miss her."

Red hair? What if it's…my stomach drops. My ears are on fire, a ringing echoes through my head.

Carson said she had a connection to Crawford and

Company. Is it the same woman? My redhead is the cupcake woman?

I knew she seemed slightly familiar and now the truth is hitting me like a ton of bricks, and it all makes perfect sense. The picture I'd seen wasn't the best and it was black and white so it's not shocking I didn't recognize her. No wonder she was so nervous.

And when did I start thinking of her as mine? I shake my head like the motion will shake away the thought along with the shock numbing my brain cells.

The phone beeps in my ear with another incoming call, jarring me from my thoughts. "I gotta go," I say to Carson and hit my phone to accept the call from Ava.

"Hey. Everything alright?" I ask distractedly.

"Yeah, we're fine. You'll be home for dinner, right?"

It takes me a few long moments to register her sentence, my mind still reeling over the fact that the woman I kissed and the food truck owner are one and the same. It has to be her. Doesn't it? There's more than one redhead in New York City, but the odds of it being someone else...

"Yes. I'll be there in about an hour and a half."

"Good. Emma misses you."

I smile. Ava likes to use Emma to explain her own feelings on things.

"I'll make something good," I say distractedly.

"Can we have ice cream?"

"Maybe after dinner."

"Can we have pancakes for dinner?"

"Do you ever want to eat anything that isn't sugar?"

"Ugh, fine." She hangs up.

Teenagers. I stop in front of the building and click over to my schedule to make sure I've remembered the address correctly.

I stare up at the sign and then back at my phone at the address in my schedule, 46 Hester Street. Yep. This is the right place. But this isn't like Sonic Yoga or the Om Factory.

It's the Meow Palace. Cat yoga?

An image flashes in my mind of Carson grinning when I agreed to take this yoga class. I'm going to kill him.

I want to turn around and run, but I can't. I know she's in there and I have to get this resolved. If I don't, Oliver might pull out and I need him. I've already sunk too much into this venture myself and if Oliver doesn't invest, it will fail and failure is not an option. And also, a much larger part of me wants to see her again. Wants to see her reaction when she realizes that I know the truth.

I step in the direction of the building right as a redhead in black pants and dark blue, fitted sweater walks in front of me, opening the door and disappearing inside. Her hair was pulled back but....

The door shuts on a whisper and my heart rate accelerates like mixer set on high.

I'm a statue on the sidewalk, the sight I just witnessed replaying in my mind like a video on a loop. Dark red hair, pulled up in a messy bun of the same shade.

It *is* her.

Even though the last thing I want to do is enter the Meow Palace, knowing that my redhead is inside compels my feet to move of their own accord and a few seconds later, I'm through the door.

There's a "Beware of Cat" mat at my feet. The floor is all hard grey, but it's contrasted with soft pillows strewn about, along with colorful shelves, cat houses, and a smiling receptionist.

"Welcome to the Meow Palace," the chipper teenager behind the desk welcomes me. "Are you here for the yoga class?"

"Yes."

She sets some forms in front of me with a pen. She's talking, explaining what to expect. But I'm only half listening while she tells me the rules, how to sanitize my hands, and where to put my shoes and coat.

I sign the waiver, wondering if I've lost my mind. First, I kiss some woman without even knowing her name, and now I'm stalking her into a cat thing. I don't even like cats.

She points out where to go and I make my way in the direction indicated.

I enter at the back of the room, my eyes immediately lasering to the only person with red hair in the entire place. She's setting up her mat near the front, her back to me.

People meander between us, settling in on brightly colored mats, talking to each other and stretching out. Cats circle the space, some laying around cleaning themselves, others playing with cat toys like a string on a stick.

The redhead turns, her profile exposed, and my stomach flips in awareness. My heart lurches and sets up a riotous rhythm.

There isn't even a sliver of doubt now. It's most definitely her.

She's sitting cross-legged on a purple mat, petting an orange tabby while it rubs a head on her knee.

I put my mat down in the back of the room next to an elderly gentleman. There are at least a dozen more people sitting or loitering around the space, but my focus is entirely on the woman in the front.

Scarlett Jackson. My redhead is the cupcake woman who has been avoiding me for weeks. I mull over our interaction through a new lens. How she saw me and immediately almost choked to death. I thought it was embarrassment from being caught in such a weird situation, but she must have known who I was.

A blonde enters from a side door, someone else I recognize—Bethany Connell, from the charity event. She waves at Scarlett and sets up her mat next to her.

Mildred. I shake my head.

I'm an idiot.

Bethany is clearly the connection between Scarlett and Crawford and Company.

The instructor comes in, a short, thin man with messy dark hair and enough energy to power Upper Manhattan vibrating off him. "Hello friends!"

The room erupts into cheers while the instructor bounces around offering greetings and air kisses at random.

A small gray cat paws at my knee, and I surreptitiously push it away. The older gentleman next to me frowns in my direction.

"Alright cat lovers, let's get warmed up. Now remember, be careful of the fur-babies roaming the room! Be aware of your surroundings and use gentle movements. If you need to stretch or kick behind you, make sure one of our *paw-some* friends isn't in the way. You can follow along as I go through the routine, but at any time feel free to rest and pet our cat family. Now let's get it started!"

I follow the instructions and guidance of the teacher and try not to stare at Scarlett too much. While I'm in the Downward-Facing Dog position, the small gray cat traces its tail around my leg and then collapses underneath me, rolling back and exposing its furry belly without any fear, like nothing in the world could hurt him.

I should be angry. All her blushing and fumbling and choking was because she expected me to recognize her. But instead she…she was interesting. And she kissed me.

"This all about joy and love and feeling purr-ific!"

Normally, I would find a way to use this to my advantage. Make her uncomfortable or find a way to use it against her to achieve my own ends.

But I'm not angry. When I stop to analyze the feelings making my heart race and my stomach flip, I'm more intrigued than anything else.

But still, I can't let her ruin my plans. There is too much riding on it. I need to nip all this in the bud and get her truck away from my space. I can't afford for Oliver to see another roadblock and use it as an excuse to kill our deal.

The gray cat rolls away just in time for me to follow along, moving from downward dog to cobra. I watch Scarlett going through the same motions, neatly avoiding the orange tabby lounging near her elbow.

Her body glides through the poses with ease and fluid movements and I want to run my hands along those same curves. I know what her body feels like, pressed against mine. The memory makes my temperature rise, and it isn't the yoga getting me hot.

The rest of the class is interminable for me, but everyone else is having fun.

"Okay friends, it's time to cool down with some light petting." His grin is just on the other side of maniacal.

I clear my throat. Surely, he could have come up with a better turn of phrase.

"Follow my lead and stretch in place or pet a furry friend nearby. Scientific studies have shown petting our animal brethren can reduce blood pressure, release relaxation hormones, and cut your stress. Pet the pussies!"

I wince.

The gray tabby still lingering around my feet swats at my ankle.

The instructor bends over and hands him to me. "This little guy really likes you!" His smiling face meets mine and then falters only slightly at my expression. I must appear less intimidating than normal.

"His name is Spike and he's one of our newest babies. Here." He thrusts him at me.

I have no choice. I take the cat, holding him awkwardly in front of me. His body curls around my hand, hind legs latching onto my forearm while he ferociously attacks my fingers with little nubby teeth.

The instructor laughs. "Aw. I think he's teething. Here. Hold him close." He pushes him against my chest and then moves on to the person next to me.

I watch the kitten nibble on my finger for a moment before glancing up to see where Scarlett is.

Our gazes lock across the room. Recognition rolls over her like a bleaching wave, her mouth drops, and her features whiten, eyes wide. Her gaze makes a sharp dart toward the door.

Already planning to flee, are we? Not this time.

I press my lips together when they threaten to curve up.

Before she can bolt, I stalk in her direction, stopping at the edge of her mat, blocking any possible escape. "Scarlett."

Her mouth pops open. She's not wearing lipstick this time.

Not that she needs it, her lips are soft pink and I wonder if that color appears anywhere else on her body. Fighting the desire tightening my stomach, I step a little closer.

"We need to talk."

Chapter Six

I THINK EVERY WOMAN SHOULD HAVE A BLOWTORCH.
 –Julia Child

Scarlett

HE'S HOLDING A KITTEN.

A young gray cat with fluffy fur sticking out every-where. The kitten is attacking his finger with his little chomp chomp chompers and Guy…he doesn't really notice.

It's quite the study in contrasts, Guy standing there staring at me like the overlord of Hell seeking to torture one of the eternally damned, while a cute little furball gnaws on him with the most adorable look of intensity on his tiny face.

I strangle back laughter.

Guy's head tilts, watching me with hooded eyes.

I can't think straight with a handsome man standing in front of me holding a kitten. He's wearing workout clothes, but to call them just workout clothes is an insult to shoulders everywhere. The shirt outlines his broad chest and lean waist, and those sweatpants….

But what stops me and effectively kills the emerging laughter are his lips.

I still remember them. Warm and strong and assured, and his tongue—gah, the memories fly through my mind, scrambling my brain.

That's it. I'm broken. My brain is broken.

It's the only explanation for what pops out of my mouth.

"You kissed me." The words emerge like an accusation.

"You kissed me back. Actually." His eyes search mine. "You kissed me first. But you said it was my fault right before you did it." He considers me carefully, the evil scowl has disappeared, replaced with amusement that makes his eyes glint with evil hellfire.

I did do that and say that, dang it.

"It's not my fault you could charm the dogs off a meat truck."

His gaze warms by a single degree—the only indication my words had any small effect on him—and then his eyes flick to my mouth.

Maybe more than a small effect.

I nip that thought right in the bud. He's everything I don't want. Controlling, arrogant, a complete jerk. I don't go for jerks, not anymore. Been there, done that, got the t-shirt that says, "I went to Jerk Land and all I got was this stupid t-shirt."

"You're the food truck owner," he says.

"Um . . ." Dang it. Caught out, times two.

"Don't try to deny it, I came here because I knew you'd be here."

"Are you stalking me now?"

"I wouldn't have to if you'd stop avoiding me."

Movement to the side distracts us both.

"Hi! Nice to see you again." Bethany waves a little sheepishly.

Awkward silence. They're both staring at me.

I find my tongue. "Bethany, this is, uh, Guy Chapman."

She nods. "Yeah, I know."

One of Guy's eyebrows lifts in a sardonic arch. "Mildred?" he asks her.

She flushes. "Oh, ha, ha, right. Well you know, I can't give out the name of a friend to a virtual stranger. That way lies murder. Even if it is at a charity event and even if I did hire you to cater. It's always people you know, you know? And I didn't know you knew each other already.... But if that's the case," her gaze flicks back and forth between the two of us. "Why did you ask me what her name was the other night if you know each other already?"

"It's been a while since we were formally introduced," I explain in a rush. My face is hot and I can feel Guy's eyes on me like a laser beam of interest and confusion.

"Huh. Okay, well you're being a weirdo right now, which makes me want to find out even more. So, Guy, we are heading out to this great dumpling place around the corner and would you like to join—?"

"He can't," I interject. "He's very busy, I'm sure."

Bethany rolls her eyes at me. "Can he speak? Because it seems like you're doing all the talking for him."

"He can speak. He can even participate in conversations in third person about him and wipe his ass with one hand."

Bethany laughs and I stare at him. He has a sense of humor? It's like he's suddenly turned into a turnip.

The instructor comes over and sweeps Bethany into some conversation and now I'm alone with Guy. I mean, we're in a room full of people, and Bethany is only a few feet away, but the way he's staring at me and the awareness of his proximity…it feels like we're the only ones in the room.

"Why didn't you tell me who you were?" he asks, his green-eyed gaze intense but his tone perfunctory. Completely in contrast with the formerly bitey little kitty, who is no longer on the attack. In fact, he's snuggled up against Guy's chest, eyes drooping, his purring rumble filling the space between us like a little motor.

"Does it matter?"

"Yes."

"If you must know, I thought you would be mean to me."

It's the truth, even though it sounds lame. Like we were two kids on a playground and I took his favorite swing and now fear his retribution.

His head tips back in surprise. "What exactly did you think I'd do?"

"I didn't really know, but I'm not good at confrontation. I was worried you'd threaten me somehow or try and scare me away from parking in my spot."

His lips purse. "That's...actually a valid concern. If I promise not to be mean, will you still hide from me?"

I think about it. "I can't promise anything."

"Why not?"

"Why don't you tell me what you've been dying to say, and we'll go from there?"

"Fine." He runs a soft finger over the head of the cat snoozing in his arms and says, "I want you to park your truck somewhere else." And then as an afterthought. "Please."

"No."

His eyes are penetrating and bright and focused right on me, like nothing else exists. "How much?"

I blink under his hard stare, confused. "How much what?"

"How much *money*?" he enunciates, as if I'm very, very slow.

He thinks he can pay me to leave. "You can't just throw money at me and expect—"

"What about ten thousand dollars?"

My mouth pops open. "You can't be serious. I don't own the space. I'm renting a small section." For a great price from a deal I got because of my friendship with Bethany and the Crawford's, which I'm sure he must have figured out by now.

"I know. But I would like to purchase it and I don't think the owner will sell unless you leave willingly."

"You got that damn straight," Bethany pops back into the conversation. "Although technically, it's not mine either, but I'm sleeping with one of the owners." She winks.

Guy stares at her for a second and then faces me. "Well, what about it? Ten thousand dollars, free and clear, and all you have to do is find somewhere else to park."

It's not a small amount of money. But in New York City, it's not enough.

Real estate costs are bad enough, but food trucks are almost worse. They are insane to try and park in the city —one of the reasons I almost didn't pursue this venture at all. Some trucks are out parking at 1 a.m. just to get a decent spot, and breaking a law is almost a certainty. You can't park in a metered space, or within 200 feet of a school, or within 500 feet of a public market and the list goes on. One vendor told me he paid $12,000 in parking tickets and fees in a month. Bethany finding this unused space in a decent and legal area was the only reason I could start the truck in the food place. And still, I have to cater on the side to make ends meet.

"You and I both know that's not enough."

His eyes are locked on mine. "Is there anything I can do to entice you to leave?"

"No."

His jaw firms. "What if I find an alternate location for you that's just as good?"

"Like where?"

"I don't know yet."

I shake my head. "I like my spot."

"I need it."

"That's not my problem."

His voice is firm and unyielding, just like his face. "I can make it a problem."

"Why would you do that?"

"I am turning that area into a high-class, exclusive dining experience. I want to use the lot as part of the plan, and no one will want to see a trashy truck selling inferior desserts while they're dining in luxury."

And there it is. All cold calculation and arrogance. Except for the kitten in his hand that opens its little mouth in a yawn and regards me with half-closed drowsy eyes.

"Sorry if my cupcakes offend your delicate sensibilities, but you aren't the boss of me." The words are pushed out through gritted teeth. "You don't own the world. Not everyone is going to cave to your demands because you snap your fingers and say so."

The corner of one lip tilts and even though I've been wondering if he ever smiles, I don't even want to see it. I want to punch it.

I poke him in the chest next to where the cat is snoozing. "It's your fault I got fired last year and no restaurants would hire me. For Goodness Cakes is my only hope and you will not take that from me, too."

A slight crease forms between his brows. "What are you talking about?" He glances over to where Bethany is talking to someone and then back. "You said we'd been introduced before. Is that true?"

Anger is a simmering boil in my veins while I stare at

him. He really doesn't remember. "You still don't recognize me."

He stares, hard. Eyes roving over my face. "We haven't met. Not since before the other night. I would remember you."

"Picture me holding a blowtorch. Maybe that will spark your memory."

He blinks rapidly. Stares at me in confusion. Then his eyes widen, oh so slightly. "You're that chef."

"*That* chef. Right. That's me."

He shakes his head. "It's been years since the…incident. You can't expect me to remember every aspiring chef I interview."

"Because so many of them try to set you on fire?"

His eyes brighten and his mouth twitches. Is he going to laugh? "I probably repressed the memory. Should I send you my therapy bills?"

"Was that a joke?"

"No." But his eyes are still alight with humor.

"It hasn't been years," I insist. "It's been less than a year."

He stares me down, but I stare right back.

"You were wearing a hat," he says finally.

The comment is so random it throws me off for a moment. "What?"

"That day. Your hair was covered by a chef's hat."

"Oh. What does that have to do with anything?"

The intensity of his gaze softens for a few seconds, like he's dazing out but then shakes his head and snaps back to focus. "Nothing. It doesn't matter. The point is that you need to find another location for your truck, and I am going to make sure it happens, one way or the other. I'm stubborn and I have a lot of resources."

Frustration sinks into me like cat's claws on a couch. "You don't understand. You blackballed me, and I had no power to go against it. And now you're just going to do it again? You're a legend in the industry."

His eyes widen slightly at the backhanded compliment, but I can't stop the words from continuing to spill out, the frustration and anger from the last year giving me the bravery and the stupidity to speak with truth.

"I was just starting out. I'm still starting out. I made a mistake, but you nearly ruined me over it. When you use your power for evil instead of good you are doing your part to limit the voice of others. Besides, cupcakes have as much value as escargot. You might have more resources than me and you might do your best to get rid of me and you might even succeed. But I will fight you till the end. Not because I'm stubborn, too, but because I have no choice."

He's glowering at me, expression inscrutable. Something flickers through his eyes though and I can't quite tell if it's respect or pity. Then he speaks. "I don't want to see you on my street next week."

Anger has escalated from a simmer to a downright inferno inside me. "Then don't look in my direction. Problem solved."

His voice turns snappish. "You really want to fight me on this?"

"Are you always such a butt-sniffing turd nugget?"

He sputters for a second, waking up the cat in his arms. "I'm not sure what's more insulting, the reference to excrement or the fact that you're pairing your inferior food with mine."

"Go piss up a rope."

"You have frosting in your hair."

My mouth pops open, eyes blinking too rapidly. Mostly because, well, he's likely right. I usually have frosting, flour, powdered sugar, or something on me. I mean, it's not exactly uncommon for chocolate chips to fall out of my bra at night when I'm getting in the shower.

But still. I can't stand him, his smoldery assholery, or the fact that he's still holding that damn adorable kitten.

I can't do it anymore. Blindly, I turn and push past the people still lingering in the room. My vision is a red haze of exasperation and helplessness. What he said was true. He could probably shut me down with no more than a snap of his fingers, and I'll have no power against him.

I'm on the sidewalk and halfway down the block before Bethany catches up with me. I'm so steaming mad I almost forgot about our dinner plans. I feel like I could angry-walk all the way across the Williamsburg Bridge. It's around here somewhere, I'm sure of it.

"Scarlett! Slow down!" She catches up to me, panting to keep up. "I have your sweater." She hands me the garment and I shrug it on, shoving my hands into the holes with more force than necessary.

"What happened with that guy, Guy?" She snorts. "Guy, guy. Ugh what an awful name. But he is kinda hot, he's got that whole sexy glower thing going on. It's not really my bag, I much prefer hunky footballer types, but you know that." She puts a hand on my shoulder, and we stop in the middle of the sidewalk. "You want to talk about it?"

I take a deep breath to try and lower my blood pressure. There might be actual flames coming out of my ears.

"It's a long story."

"Good. You can tell me at dinner because it's literally right here." She stops in front of a small storefront with a red awning.

We walk into the narrow restaurant space—hardly big enough for the counter and two small tables with rickety chairs. Bethany orders us enough dumplings, spring rolls, sesame pancakes, and soup to feed half of Manhattan but I don't say anything.

I grab us some waters, napkins, plastic forks, and chopsticks from a counter to the side. I take a few deep breaths, regret my life decisions, and think of all the things I should have said to Guy when I had the chance while simultaneously hoping I never see him again.

When we take our seats, my aim is distraction. "So, how's work? Has Mr. Crawford really retired or is he still poking around being obnoxious?"

Bethany gives me the side-eye. "My soon-to-be father-in-law has mellowed in the manipulative ass-face department, however that is not the topic at hand. Yet." She points at me. "Time to spill. What was up with all that intense staring and tension? I couldn't tell if you were going to rip off his head or his clothes, but since you were running down the sidewalk like the hounds of hell were after you, I'm presuming it's the latter."

I huff out a laugh. "The head coming off, yes, the

clothes, not likely. I'd rather sleep with an ornery porcu-
pine than Guy Chapman. It would be less likely to stab
me multiple times."

Except every time I'm around him I want to make out
with him, but that's beside the point and irrelevant now.
The fact that he's a giant turd helps make him less attractive. Sort of.

She laughs. "That's cute, but not cute enough to get
you out of this conversation. You already avoided me
once at the gala when you saw him, and I knew I should
have pushed you harder then. Let's start at the beginning.
How do you know him? And why have I not heard about
this?"

*Because I don't like telling everyone my embarrassing moments
when they'll likely witness it for themselves eventually?*

But this is Bethany. She's the least judgmental person I
know. So I tell her. "You know how Gwen and I were in
Page Seven that one time?"

She nods. "Yeah, when that piece of crap date tried to
roofie you and Gwen saw it and you guys totally got him
arrested like a couple of badass bitches? I remember."

"Shortly after all that, Guy was doing interviews for a
new restaurant. They are notoriously hard to even get a
chance to try. You have to be a big name or know someone. The person doing the hiring recognized me from the
story with Gwen, and I got an interview. Which means, I
got to cook with Guy. It would have been the opportunity
of a lifetime except I ruined it."

"What did you do?"

"I sort of," I grimace and say the words quickly, like
ripping off a band-aid, "Set him on fire."

Bethany gapes at me, opened mouth for a few long seconds, and then she bursts out laughing.

The woman at the counter calls out her name and Bethany gets up to collect the order, still laughing her head off.

When she comes back with our tray, I help her set out the items on the teeny table.

"It's not funny!"

"It is more than funny, it's the best thing I've heard all year. How have I not heard this story?" She grabs the Sriracha and squeezes some onto her plate. "Please tell me everything."

I sigh and fiddle with my chopsticks. "You haven't heard it because it's not exactly something I like to talk about. Basically, I was putting the finishing touches on a crème brûlée, and I…tripped."

"So, you were torching a dessert, presumably standing in place and you, what, decided to run around holding a flammable? That doesn't make sense. And that's not like you. As crazy as you can get everywhere else, you're meticulous in the kitchen."

I squirm. "Okay, so it was less tripping and more of a…startle."

Her brows lift and she waits for more.

"He came up next to me to observe, and I didn't see him. Then he startled me, and I sort of turned into him."

"What startled you?"

Bethany *would* needle in on the one topic I want to avoid the most.

I glance around the small space—there's one couple ordering at the counter and no one is paying us any mind, but still. I lean in and lower my voice. "I have a Guy Chapman problem."

Bethany pops a dumpling in her mouth and chews with a shrug. "What does that mean?"

"It means that whenever he's around, I get crazy."

"Like, talking to apples in the grocery store crazy? Or rip off all your clothes and throw yourself at him crazy?"

I fidget with my chopsticks. "The second one. It's like he has this effect on me that I can't control."

Bethany nods decisively. "You should totally bone him. Set him on fire the metaphorical way instead of the literal way."

I grimace. "I didn't set him completely on fire, that was a slight exaggeration. I burned his chef's jacket, though."

"That doesn't sound too bad."

"His lucky chef's jacket."

"Oh."

I stare down at the sesame pancakes on my plate, like they'll make the story any less true. "It was ruined. And he's known to be a bit of a perfectionist. Obviously, I didn't get the job, but it was worse than that. He bad-mouthed me to everyone. And then I lost my job, which was crappy anyway, but no one else would hire me. Seriously. I couldn't get a job making sandwiches at the bodega in Hunts Point."

She takes bite of food before responding. "Okay, so you guys have all this awkward past history, but from where I was standing, there was also a lot of sizzle. He's hot. And he's a chef, like you. You're basically soulmates and you should totally bone him."

"These sesame pancakes are fantastic." I take another bite. Perfectly crisp on the outside, soft on the inside and stuffed with chives and greens.

"Stop trying to avoid the subject."

"Fine. We are not soulmates. Yes, he's a chef, but in my book, that's strike one. Strike two, he's too important and well-known and rich. He would never slum it with the likes of me, and I wouldn't want him to because strike three, he's a major turd."

"Being important and rich is not a deal-breaker. And no one is serious all the time. He made that joke, where he referred to himself in third person? That was self-deprecatory and funny. And I saw him watching you, that was more heat than hate. Maybe he doesn't mean to be an ass all the time, he just has resting fuck face."

I laugh. "What is that?"

"It's like," she waves a hand, "resting bitch face, but for dudes."

"You didn't hear the rest of the conversation. He's trying to make me move from my spot because it's interfering with his fancy businesses. He called me inferior."

She takes a drink of her water. "He said you were inferior?"

"Okay, well maybe he didn't call me inferior directly. He said my food was inferior."

"But—"

"I don't want to talk about him anymore. Can we discuss something else?"

"Fine. But since he's not Mr. Right or even Mr. Right Now, let me know if you want me to dig up any dirt on him. I know high people in low places. Or whatever."

Our conversation moves on to our jobs, Bethany's boyfriend, the upcoming holidays, and other various and sundry, but part of my mind lingers back, stuck on an ornery chef with bright green eyes and the means to destroy me.

Chapter Seven

THE DISCOVERY OF A NEW DISH DOES MORE FOR THE happiness of the human race than the discovery of a star.
  –Jean Anthelme Brillat-Savarin

Guy

AS SOON AS CARSON RETURNS, my entire body tenses and I want to leap up and demand answers. I force myself into stillness, disturbed to realize it's requiring a concerted effort to act unaffected and normal.

I have not been waiting for him all morning to return with my latest request.

I have not been thinking about a beautiful redhead for the last week.

And I have not been thinking about kissing a problematic baker with frosting in her hair and a temper that makes her eyes spark and chest heave.

Maybe if I keep lying to myself, those statements will become true.

"Just leave it there." I motion to the empty space at the corner of my desk. Like the item is unimportant.

Carson sets the small box down and I wave him away, typing on my computer and focusing like I'm in the middle of something serious.

Maybe I've been thinking about her a little. Maybe I thought about it all day yesterday and made a point to come up with plans to see her again, even though I have other, more important things to worry about, and I could probably drive her and her little food truck away without having to actually see her again.

But her words keep playing like a loop in my mind, *when you use your power for evil instead of good you are doing your part to limit the voice of others*, and even though my initial reaction was immediate and unequivocal denial, in retrospect I can't help but consider, is she right? Even a little bit?

My mind plays over every employee I've ever fired or had harsh words for. The number is substantial.

Shame slithers through me like an insidious snake, biting at will. I've always existed in this bubble of my own making, ignoring anyone and anything outside it, including people and situations I'd shoved away myself. It allowed me to pick and choose how I perceived my own actions and everyone outside the bubble didn't matter or exist. But what Scarlett said…maybe she's right.

I wait until Carson is on the phone, scheduling deliveries or something before I reach for the cupcake.

There's a sticker holding the top fold together. For

Goodness Cakes, written in a rainbow swirl of color. I pry it off and open the delicately folded box slowly.

The flavor is written in script on the inside. Rhett Velvet. Red velvet chocolate chip with a butter crème ganache.

There are three miniature cakes in the box. We engage in the stare down, the cupcakes and me.

I have no choice but to blink first. It's the details that give away the skill behind the ridiculous name and frivolous packaging.

It's perfectly arranged in the little box, and the frosting isn't marred or smudged at all. It's hard to believe this flawless confection came from the same woman who set me on fire and can't even keep her clothes and hair in order, just in general. At least, not the two times I've seen her.

I want it to be bad.

I want it to be good.

I sigh and take a bite.

The flavors melt on my tongue, a flawless balance sweet, savory, and light. It's perfect. As someone who requires perfection in all things, I can recognize it when I taste it. Despite what I told her, cupcakes might be simple, but there's an art to all cooking and we both know it. There's something surprising in the frosting. A hint of cayenne, I think. Not enough to give it any kind of heat, just a slight smoky essence.

"Carson!" I call.

"Yes?" He's already at the door.

"Did you try one?"

He hesitates and glances away.

I stare at him. I know he's been over there nearly every day, and it's not like I'm going to get mad at him. But still, he won't meet my gaze. This again. Am I really such an ogre? I mean, I know I am, it's part of a carefully culti-vated image, but it's also how I get things done and how I've made a name for myself, which now creates hundreds of jobs for others. But still. Have I become immune to myself?

"Yes," he says finally.

"Did you have the same?" I hold up what's left of the cake in my hand.

"No." His eyes shift away again. "There was a special today."

I lift a brow.

He smirks. "It's called, 'Guy Chapman is a Butt-Sniffing Douche Double Chocolate with Nougat'."

I press my lips together. "Really. That's quite a mouthful."

His brows lift at my response and I work to keep my expression blank.

His smirk rolls into an all-out grin. "She used a dark chocolate crème anglaise. The cake was good, but the nougat filling, it was inspired. You have to admit it's kind of funny."

"Right. Funny." I will not smile.

When I don't say anything further, Carson steps away, moving back toward his desk.

"Carson," I bark.

He steps back to the threshold, waiting for me to continue.

"Do you think I'm mean?"

A few beats of silence pass while he stares at me, wide eyed. "Are you for real?"

My teeth clench. "I wouldn't ask if I weren't."

He shifts from one foot to another. "Well, it's really kind of subjective."

I make a derisive sound. "You never quibble over semantics. Tell me straight."

"You know people are scared of you."

That's not an answer. "Do you think I use my influence for evil instead of good?"

"No. I think you're dedicated to success and you know how many people rely on you. You might be demanding, but you know you have to be strong enough for everyone and you demand no more than you demonstrate."

For some reason, his words don't make me feel any better. Being an unemotional prick doesn't make me strong. Scarlett laid herself bare right in front of me, showing me all her weakest spots. But that didn't make her fragile or pathetic. Showing her vulnerable underside to me, her current enemy, was probably the bravest thing I've ever witnessed. I've always lived under a hard and fast rule of flaunting only competence, but showing weakness takes real courage. Real strength.

I consider Carson, his perfect suit and manicured moustache. "You've never been scared of me. Not even during your first interview."

One shoulder lifts in a half shrug. "My dad is six foot five, a two-hundred and fifty-pound former collegiate linebacker and he loves Jesus. I had to have a conversation with him about how much I enjoy penis. Nothing scares me after that."

I nod.

I don't want to do it, not really, but I need that slice of real estate in order to continue to pay my staff, Carson included. It's unfortunate Scarlett is going to get caught in the crossfire but it's inevitable. There is more on the line than she realizes and there are things out of my control. Like Oliver.

"Get Officer Jackson on the phone." Jerome is a friend from high school he owes me a favor because I catered his niece's sweet sixteen last year.

Carson regards me, his expression carefully blank. "Are you sure?"

"There aren't any other choices."

He disappears from the doorway and a few seconds later, he's on the phone.

I take another bite of the Rhett Velvet and can't help but wonder what the 'Guy Chapman is a butt-sniffing douche double chocolate with nougat' cupcake tastes like. I almost wish I could try one.

"Funny," I murmur. "Clever marketing, too." Especially from my employees, apparently.

"I've got Officer Jackson," Carson calls.

I lean back in my chair and pick up the phone. Scarlett said she doesn't have a choice. Well, neither do I. Not really.

WE'RE on the couch watching Mr. Bean, one of Emma's favorite shows, when my phone rings.

"Jerome," I answer. "Tell me something good."

Emma reaches over and pokes me in the mouth. I swipe her hand away and she grins at me then points at the TV.

Mr. Bean is in a karate class, shoving the teacher over and rolling him in a mat.

Jerome speaks in my ear. "Man, you didn't tell me what a piece Scarlett was. You could warn a brother."

"A piece?"

Emma reaches for my face again and I stand to avoid her. Ava sits on my other side and she swats at my thigh. "You're ruining the show, this is Emma's favorite part."

I sneak off into the next room to have the conversation in relative peace.

Jerome continues. "She is something else. She told me she was nervous because I might have to cuff her. Gave me all kinds of ideas."

I have a sudden and visceral vision of punching Jerome right in the face. Clenching my teeth together, I ignore his statement and force out the question. "Did you check the permit?"

"Yeah, it all checked out. She's clean. Not much I could do, except get her number."

"You got her number? You were supposed to scare her, not hit on her." Heat flushes up the back of my neck. Blood starts a low simmer in my veins.

"She's gorgeous and she bakes. It's a no-brainer."

"You're a no-brainer." Great. Now I've turned into a middle-schooler.

Jerome laughs. "Does that mean she's off-limits? Bro code?"

I take a deep breath and glance into the living room

where Emma and Ava are watching Mr. Bean, the light from the TV playing over their faces. Emma laughs at something, accompanied by the laugh track emanating from the TV. "No. She's not off limits. Call her all you want." The words are forced out through clenched teeth.

Jerome, the dick, laughs harder. "Cool, man, maybe I will. I'll let you know how it goes."

"You do that."

"You coming to poker night next week?"

"I'll have to check my schedule."

My old friends from college have a long-standing poker night, which I've never made. My schedule is too crammed. All my time is spent between work and taking care of the girls.

"Uh huh. I know what that means. You take care, man. And, hey, let me know if you change your mind and decide you like cupcakes after all, okay?"

I hang up on his chuckles and go back to the living room, resuming my spot between my sisters.

Emma pats my head gracelessly and leans against my side, a comforting warmth.

It bothers me more than it should that the annoying baker gave her number to my friend.

It continues to bother me through two more episodes of Mr. Bean and getting the girls ready for bedtime, and even leaks into the next morning.

I get to Decadence an hour late, and For Goodness Cakes is parked outside, mocking me with its colorful visage, happy and bright red and glaring. The generator hums, sending a corresponding drumming through my veins.

Once inside my office, I try to focus on work, but everything takes forever because I can't get her out of my mind. The things she said, her dark blue eyes, her sincerity, and that damn delicious cupcake.

By the time dinner service is about to begin, I'm ready to give up. I can't let my emotions interfere with business but the need to see her is like an itchy scab that begs to be scratched—but you know if you do, you'll just bleed.

And that's why, for the first time in years, I break my routine. I should be here, making sure everything runs smoothly for the intimate seating tonight, but I can't take it anymore.

Standing, I grab my coat from the rack behind my desk and stalk out.

Laughter and the clank of dishes fill the kitchen, chefs talking over the running sink as the staff cleans dishes and preps ingredients.

"You asshole!" Beatrice throws her apron at Joseph, but they both freeze when they see me passing through.

I don't have to say anything; they immediately start moving back to their stations, leaving the apron discarded on the floor. I pick it up and a lump of something orange and gooey slides out.

"What's this?" I ask.

Joseph laughs, the sound high pitched with nerves, "It's just a prank. I'll clean it up." He scrambles in front of me and kneels on the floor with a rag, scrubbing vigorously.

My lips twist. Kitchen pranks. They happen everywhere and normally I might snap at them to make better

use of paid time and not waste my eggs but this time...
they've given me an idea.

"It's fine." Without further thought, I hand him the
apron and grab a couple of eggs from the carton on the
counter on my way out of the kitchen, sliding them carefully into the front pocket of my jacket, my mind already
across the street.

"What's with him?" Someone says behind me in a
shocked voice, as I'm leaving, but I don't pay them any
mind. I've got a chef to chat with.

The truck window is closed, but light spills through the
cracks. I shove my hands into my coat huff out a visible
breath into the freezing night air. A lone snowflake drifts
in an erratic pattern in front of me on a bitterly cold
breeze, an omen of more to come. The girls will be happy
if we get a good snowfall before Christmas. They love
sledding in Central Park.

I round the red shiny truck to the back door and
knock sharply three times.

No sounds of movement from within.

Maybe she's avoiding me again.

But then she opens the door and I step back in
surprise.

"Oh, it's you." She wipes her hands on a bright
orange dishtowel and considers me with a scowl. "I
thought maybe this time you called your momma on me
when your cop buddy wasn't enough."

"That would be quite the feat for me to accomplish."

"Why?"

"My mother passed five years ago."

"Oh. Sorry." She peers over my head out the door.

"It's fixing to snow. You better—," she eyeballs me and then comes to a decision, "—come in before you catch your death."

I step into a gentle heat that smells like vanilla and sugar. I glance around the space. My first thought is warm and cozy. And clean. There's a double oven on one side with a coffee/tea set up and storage for food and supplies. She's not wearing her apron and I locate it hanging on the back of the door I came through.

She turns away, wiping down an already clean counter. "What did you want?"

"Just wondering if tomorrow's special will be as interesting as the one from the other day."

"I don't know, you'll have to find out from your spies." She turns around, folding her arms over her chest and leaning back against the counter.

"I've got some suggestions, actually."

"This should be good."

"What about, 'Guy Chapman has impeccable apple creme cinnamon buns'?"

"Not sure it would sell. You're lucky all I've done is name a cupcake after you, considering what you pulled."

I shrug it off. "It was just a cop. Would you rather I called the health inspector?"

She turns around to face me, her shoulders tense. "Do your worst. I have all my permits and I follow code to the letter."

I glance around, frowning in judgment, a move that normally makes people nervous. Scarlett isn't deterred, and watches me in stony silence.

I try a different tact, taking a step closer in the small

space so we're only a couple feet apart. "You know this is all giving me even more publicity. Thanks for helping me out."

She scowls. "If it was really helping you out, you wouldn't be here harassing me."

"I'm not harassing you. I'm just here to talk to a neighbor. Being neighborly. Maybe I need a cup of sugar."

"This is intimidation tactics." She points at me. "I know your methods. And you're sending your spies over here and sampling my goods."

"Sampling your goods?" I lift a brow. I only wish I could sample a bite of any part of her. The small taste the other night was not enough.

I freeze at the thought. Where did that come from? I absolutely cannot sample any of her goods, not that she would offer again.

But I can't stop staring. There's bit of something on her collarbone, a swipe of flour, and it inexplicably makes me want to bite her, right there. What kind of sound would she make if I did?

"Did you eat it?" she asks, after a too long silence.

I blink. What were we talking about? "Eat what?"

"One of my cupcakes."

I cross my arms over my chest, mimicking her pose across the small space. "I did."

Her mouth pops open. "You did?"

"It was too dry. The cayenne in the frosting was okay, but it might be better if you used cardamom instead."

She turns away, fumbling with a mixer on the counter. "You're full of it. That cake was perfect."

I lean over, moving quickly before she turns around again and drop the eggs into the pocket of her apron hanging at the door.

I step back quickly, just before she faces me, except I came back a bit too far and we're even closer now in the confined space.

"Is anything ever perfect?" It's all I've ever cared about, and yet "perfect" is never quite as fulfilling as it seems like it would be.

She's staring up at me, her eyes large, pupils dilated. She swallows and I watch the delicate bones of her throat move.

"Why are you here? Did you come over to try and intimidate me?"

"Is it working?"

"No. You're just making me want to best you even more."

"What are you going to do? Will you name another cupcake after me?" I want to see her eyes spark again.

"I think the idea of butt-flavored cake has worn out its welcome. I can only shock people so many times before it becomes commonplace."

I want to laugh, but I press my lips together instead. "You can't say it, can you?"

"Say what?"

"You want to call me an asshole, but you settle on insults like turd nugget and butt-flavor." I lean toward her, satisfaction filling me when her mouth parts slightly and her breath comes faster.

She's not unaffected by me; I know this, and I'm glad. I can't be the only one fighting this attraction. My own breathing is picking up speed, heart thumping a little faster. What is it about this woman that makes me want to break all my own rules?

"Some of us have manners. Were you raised in a barn?"

"Close enough."

My eyes flick to the smear of flour on her collarbone. "You have flour on you. Maybe you should wear that apron you left over there before you start baking. I think that's a health code regulation."

She groans in frustration and steps away, using my comment as an excuse to get away from me, likely, reaching for the garment. "I hate you."

"Good." Because I'm supposed to be keeping her at arm's length and not doing...whatever it is I'm doing right now.

She's blushing. Flustered. She grabs the apron and yanks it off the hook to send the eggs flying.

Chapter Eight

COOKING AND BAKING ARE BOTH PHYSICAL AND EMOTIONAL therapy.
  —Mary Berry

Scarlett

EGGS. He put eggs in my apron and now they're broken, shells littering the floor and speckled over my legs and shoes.

Startled, I freeze in shock, blinking at the egg carnage and then up at Guy.

He smiles.

"You…you…turd burglar!" I don't know what else to say. Guy Chapman played a silly prank on me. And now he's *smiling*.

Like actual smiling. With his lips and even teeth. They're nice teeth, straight and white and . . . hell's bells!

He never smiles that big. Ever. The most I've ever witnessed is a slight tilt of the lips. And it's a good thing because he has a dimple in his left cheek and his grin is more divine than tiramisu straight from Rome. Guy always has a certain magnetism, even when he's just standing there scowling, but an actual real to life smile might power the mixer on the counter—no electricity needed.

"Can you not swear?" he asks. "You know you're a grown adult and no one's here to reprimand you." The dimple is gone, disappeared along with most of my brain cells.

I can't believe he. . .

"Ugh!" I grab a piece of the gelatinous material from my shirt and throw it at him, but it doesn't go very far. The goop slips beneath my fingers and leaves a sticky trail up my arm.

Which makes him smile again. Damn him. Anger fills me with resolve.

I step in his direction, rubbing my hand in the excess egg on my person and then wiping the wetness right across his smug face.

He stares at me in shock, the eggy mess a smear of shiny substance across his cheek and chin.

In an ineffectual attempt to hide my mirth, I cup my hands over my mouth and snort into them, which just wipes more of the egg on my own face, but there's no helping it.

His frozen shock doesn't last long. He steps toward me, coming for me even as I back away, but there's nowhere to go.

Yelping, I try to escape his retribution, but my truck is smaller than a prison cell. He easily boxes me in against the counter and then, to my everlasting shock, rubs his egg-covered face against mine.

His cheek is scratchy and the egg is wet. The combination has me shrieking and laughing and struggling to get away, but his arms are like warm steel bands caging me in place.

The door slams open and we both freeze, halting mid-entanglement, and turn our heads as one toward the interruption.

Fred stands in the doorway, disposable coffee containers in each hand. It's going to be a long night and I had sent her off for reinforcements because we were out.

Guy steps away from me, wiping his face with the back of his sleeve. I straighten and clear my throat, hastily using a dry spot on my apron to wipe my own face.

"Right. Thank you for the, uh, chat and tips."

His brows lift. "Tips?"

"The um, cardamom. It's a terrible suggestion, but you know, you tried."

I turn and put my apron on the counter and then grab a rag from the rack and start wiping off the countertop again. I'll ignore him and this whole thing, pretending like none of it happened.

His voice is back to its normal snappish tone. "Right. Enjoy the eggs."

And without a goodbye, he walks out the door, nodding at Fred who watches him walk away and then turns to face me.

"What the hell was that all about?"

I shake my head in bafflement. "I don't know. He smiled."

Her brows lift. "He smiled? At you? Are you sure he wasn't having a seizure or a stroke or something?" She frowns and moves to the order window, lifting it slightly to watch him.

"He smiled at me and he...he pranked me. The old eggs in the apron trick."

She turns slowly around from the window with eyes wide, mouth open in disbelief. "Really?"

"I know. It's been awhile. I haven't been involved in a kitchen prank since culinary school." So juvenile. So unexpected. I rub my cheek where his stubble abraded it, disbelief fighting with a strange sense of arousal in my belly. I can't believe he was so...playful. That in and of itself is attractive; combined with being imprisoned in his strong arms, surrounded by his heat and smell.... Despite the stickiness, I wouldn't mind if it had lasted longer. I mean, he was attacking me, yes, but there was something inherently familiar in his movements. I didn't feel threat-ened. It was...fun.

Dammit, it would be better if he'd just remained an emotionless ass. When he's playful, he's as irresistible as a chocolate shake at a burger joint.

"So, what are we gonna do about it?" Fred asks.

I unstick my tongue from the roof of my mouth. "What do you mean?"

"Um, he pranked you. You have to get him back."

"I do?" I turn away from her, grab the cloth from where I left it on the counter and wipe it on my face. An idea shimmers to life in my mind. I'm not really scared of

Guy Chapman. Not anymore. I mean, I'm scared of the attraction I feel toward him, but I can handle that. Maybe. But if I've learned anything, it's I need to stop avoiding the things—or people—that scare me. Guy isn't as scary now that I've yelled at him, been egged by him, and well, made out with him.

I meet Fred's eyes. "I mean, I do." I stand up straight. "And I have an idea. But we might need Carson." I rub my hands together. "And I know how we're going to get him to help."

Her eyes meet mine and I grin.

It. Is. On.

A FEW DAYS pass before we have a chance to set the scene to perfection. I baked a batch of hummingbird cupcakes and Fred and I are waiting for Carson to walk by. She's been using a handheld fan to blow the scent out the window.

He hasn't been by since the whole egg incident, and I don't know if it has something to do with that, or if I'm overthinking it. Probably overthinking. I do that a lot. It's like the gift that keeps giving and giving and giving.

Carson stops midstride and pivots in our direction, only stopping once his head is halfway in the order window. He breathes deeply, shutting his eyes then opening them again. "Did you make hummingbird cakes?"

"It's possible." She shrugs trying to play it off, but her smile is triumphant. "Want to come in and try them out?"

He's at the back door like a flash.

She opens the door and ushers him inside, shutting the door behind him.

"What is this?" he asks when he sees the rest of the items we've set up on the counter.

"Let me take your coat." I hold out my hand. "We're celebrating. Want a drink?"

"What. Is. All that?" His eyes are locked on the tier of cupcakes, right next to a pitcher filled with a bright yellow fluid.

Fred shrugs. "I may have bribed someone at Attaboy's to come over and make a pitcher of cocktails to go with the cake . . ."

Carson hands me his coat without even glancing in my direction. "Those bartenders make the best drinks," he breathes.

He beelines for the cupcakes and cocktails, and Fred and I exchange a triumphant smile.

An hour later, we are sitting on the floor of the food truck and more than a little tipsy. Carson is next to me, our backs to the counter, and Fred is across from us leaning back against the opposite side.

"Your cakes are the best, Scarlett." Carson leans into me, setting his head on my shoulder. "I really love you guys."

I pat him on the head. "You're an affectionate drunk."

His head lifts from my shoulder. "I'm not drunk, you are."

"Want more?" Fred asks. "I'm done. All the sugar is making my stomach feel funny and I'm tired." She stifles a yawn.

"Amateur," Carson teases and holds out his martini glass. "Yes, please." Once she's refilled his glass, he puts his head back on my shoulder, spilling some of the drink on my pants. He doesn't notice. "I'm sorry about the whole Guy trying to make you move thing. But I think he really likes you, it's just his businesses always come first. He's not the best at, you know, being a normal human."

"Really? He pranked me."

His head lifts again. "What?"

"He put eggs in my apron."

"No." He leans further back to focus on my face, his expression a mixture of confusion and shock. "He would never."

"He did," Fred confirms. "I saw it. Well, the aftermath. They were rubbing faces."

He gasps and shoves me in the shoulder. "You rubbed faces with Guy? Why are you just now telling me this?"

"We haven't seen you since then." Fred narrows her eyes at him.

"He wanted to lay low for a few days. He specifically told me not to come over here anymore or do any more espionage. I thought it was because he had a plan but. . ." He frowns in thought.

Fred and I meet eyes. She nods and then kicks Carson with her foot. "We wanted to get him back, for the pranking."

His eyes dart from Fred to me and then back again. "What? You want me to help you?"

"I don't know," I say before Fred can jump in with an emphatic affirmative. "Would you be willing to get involved? We don't want you to get in any kind of trouble."

He purses his lips in thought, and then he breaks into a grin. "One more martini and one more cupcake, and I'll do whatever you want."

Fred pulls a box from the cupboard behind her. "Good, because Scarlett wants into his office."

———

"ARE you sure you won't get fired for this?"

Decadence is dark and quiet; everyone has gone home for the night as we pass through the stainless-steel kitchen, gleaming in the emergency lights.

I'm carrying the box of goodies because Fred went home. Jack came and picked her up since the drinks went straight to her head.

"He won't fire me. He needs me too much. Besides, I think this is good for him," Carson says. "You're not doing anything mean or detrimental to his business, so he'll survive. You should have seen him the past couple of days. He's been…different."

"What do you mean?"

"He hasn't yelled at anyone. At all. The staff is so much happier. The face rubbing with you is the only thing that's changed. It's the only explanation."

He flicks on a light in the hall, leading me down a stark white hallway.

"Have you ever seen him smile? Like a big smile?" I ask.

Carson chuckles, turning us into an alcove with a

small desk and filing cabinets. There's a door leading to what must be Guy's office. Carson stops in front of the door. "Um, that's cute, honey, but he doesn't smile."

"But he does."

"He does not."

I adjust my grip on the box of goodies in my arms. "He smiled at me."

Carson puts a hand on his hip. "I have worked for the man for five years and told him every snarky joke I could come up with, and I'm hilarious. You must be lying."

"I'm not. He has a dimple."

He stares at me in shocked silence for so long, I put the box down at my feet. Finally, he nods and purses his lips. "See. I knew it. He needs you."

I stop him. "Oh no, it's not like that."

He rolls his eyes and fumbles with putting his key in the door. "You can't tell me you made him smile and then expect me to believe it doesn't mean something."

"He hates me."

"Fine, maybe it's not like true looooove," he pushes open the door, "but he likes people who stand up to him and won't let him run all over them."

"He has you."

"I am not enough. And you have better hair. And boobs. Really, the only people he lets talk to him like that are me and his sisters." He waves a hand. "Enough of that, here we go." He flicks the lights on.

I don't know what I expected of Guy's office, but in my deepest imaginings I don't think I could have come up with something so bland and sterile. It's like a doctor's office, except those will occasionally have whimsical posters or something. The walls are white, the desk is grey. There's literally nothing personal in the space—not even a single picture frame. You could probably perform open heart surgery on his desk with zero risk of infection.

"There's nothing here. I don't know if this is going to work," I tell Carson.

He moves behind Guy's desk, opening a few of the drawers. "Au contraire, mon frère. He has stuff, it's just put in its proper place."

Of course.

We spend the next thirty minutes sticking googly eyes and fake mustaches onto everything we can find. All his pens, a few mechanical pencils, a calculator, a stapler, the doorknob, the light socket, anywhere we can make look like a face. Then for the grand finale, Carson helps me affix an airhorn to his chair. As soon as he sits, he'll get a nice loud surprise.

Carson and I share a grin as he's locking up. I can't wait to find out how he reacts.

———

"NOTHING." Carson leans into the order window further and shoves his hands into his coat pockets.

"Nothing?" Fred and I repeat at the same time, our voices mingling in surprise.

We've been waiting for news all morning, but Carson didn't come over until we watched Guy leave fifteen minutes ago, stalking out the door and getting into some kind of sleek black SUV and driving off.

"It was more terrifying than if he had yelled or

reacted in some way. First thing, he sat down, the horn went off - it was loud - and he," Carson shakes his head in amazement. "He didn't. Even. Flinch!"

"Impossible."

"He didn't even say anything, just got up and examined the chair like it was expected and removed it."

"No reaction to the googly eyes, either?"

"Barely. When he saw them, there was a whisper of hesitation, and then he went right back to work."

"It's like he's not even human."

"There was one thing, though." He taps a finger on his lips.

"What is it?"

"His mouth twitched when he saw his pen with the mustache, and it wasn't the normal twist of annoyance. I think he's in love with you."

"Because his mouth twitched? You are delusional," I say.

Fred waves an impatient hand. "We need something else. But how can you prank someone who doesn't play along? We need something good."

"He didn't appear to care, but he's good at being a robot."

Fred taps the counter in frustration. "He started this whole thing. Do you think he'll come up with some retribution?"

Carson shrugs. "If he does, I'm afraid I can't share, ladies."

"Why not?" Fred asks.

"I don't take sides, honey."

They eye each other for a minute, some kind of wordless communication passing between them that makes me feel like I'm missing part of this conversation. "You helped us with our prank, you're on our side," she insists.

"I was lured to the dark side with your witchy cakes and cocktails. It doesn't count." He points at Fred's shirt, which has a picture of Darth Vader and reads, "Welcome to the Dark Side: We have cupcakes."

"You suck, Carson."

"Love you, too, Fred. I gotta get back but we'll chat soon." He blows a kiss and stalks back across the small alleyway to Decadence.

I turn to Fred. "What now?"

She coughs into her elbow a few times before responding. "I don't know." She sniffs.

"Are you okay?"

"Yeah, fine. Just allergies or something."

"Uh, Fred, it's December."

"I'm fine." She waves me off. "What's more important is anticipating Guy's next move. We have to stay one step ahead. At least. Maybe ten steps ahead."

I mull it over. "I'm having dinner with Bethany. I'll ask her. She's good at this stuff. You want to come?"

"Not this time. I'm a little tired."

"Oh, no. Still tired?" I examine her a little more closely. Is her face paler than normal? And the coughing… "Are you getting sick?"

"Absolutely not." She rubs her head and winces. "Well, maybe?"

"You should go home and rest. Do you want me to call Jack?"

"No. It's fine. He wasn't happy when he had to pick

me up the other night. He was in the middle of something at work."

I press my lips against a snarky comment. I'm not sure how I feel about Jack. Fred's been with him since they were teenagers, but something about him is bit off. He works a lot, which I can understand, but I worry about Fred, especially since they live together but their place is only in his name. If something happened between them…. It's really none of my business, though, and I am not the person to give advice about relationships, especially considering my own checkered history. And in the past, when I've made comments, Fred immediately makes it clear the topic is off-limits. She's loyal to a fault, I think.

"I can call you an Uber or something?" I offer.

"It's fine. I've got it. I'll…go home and order Pho. But maybe I shouldn't be around the cakes, just in case. Can't risk it if I am getting sick. It would be your luck for Guy to make good on his health department threat and have them show up while I'm sneezing into the batter."

"Take tomorrow off, too, just in case. I want you to feel better so you can help me with the Beatles wedding this weekend."

It was a good gig to land, based on a referral from another wedding a few months ago. It's a huge order, five hundred guests, and they have a specialized theme which means I would need to bake and decorate over fifteen hundred mini cupcakes. The mother of the bride is an editor at Women's Weekly magazine. If I do well, maybe it will lead to more catering jobs. Then I can have a bit of a cushion instead of living week to week.

But I'll also need Fred's help. I'll have to bake everything the day before so it's as fresh as possible. I already ordered stencils with little guitars and Beatle-shaped heads, shaggy hair and all, but making the fondant and cutting each piece by hand will be a lot of detailed work.

"I'm sure I'll be fine by this weekend," Fred assures me. "It's probably nothing. Just stress. Jack has been working a lot at the museum, so I've been doing as much as I can to make everything easy for him at home."

I have to bite my lip again, but I nod at Fred and then she leaves and I'm alone. It's not my place to judge, when all I have is my truck and the cakes around me.

It's enough, I tell myself, but I don't really believe it.

Chapter Nine

FOOD IS SYMBOLIC OF LOVE WHEN WORDS ARE INADEQUATE.
   −Alan D. Wolfelt

Scarlett

"YOU BETTER BE safe and invest in some condoms or something," I say to Reese on the phone at the exact moment Brent opens the door to the apartment he shares with Bethany.

He bursts out laughing and I could just die of mortification.

I hadn't even knocked yet, but I'm sure the doorman called up to let them know of my arrival.

He steps back to let me in.

My face is on fire, and Brent is still laughing.

"Reese? I just got to Bethany's but we'll talk more

later. I love you, ok bye." I hang up quickly and Brent leans in for a side hug.

"Scarlett, always a pleasure."

"Hey Brent, sorry about that, duty calls."

"That's some important duty. Bethany is in the living room." He gestures down the hall and I walk along the tiled entry and into the open spaciousness that is living in rich-person-land Manhattan. There's original artwork on the walls—one of them is a vibrant abstract my mother painted and costs more than six months of my rent—and the living room is all sleek hardwood floors and white, upscale furniture along with a giant flat screen.

Bethany's apartment is the nicest place I've ever been. And it's in Greenwich Village. I mean, Julia Roberts lives in Greenwich Village.

Bethany is on the couch, cross legged with her laptop balanced on her thighs. "You should tell Reese to put the condoms in strategic locations. That way, if the urge strikes, you're prepared no matter where you are." She winks at Brent who's still chuckling behind me.

I can't help but scan the living room. "Are you saying you have condoms hidden all over this place?"

"I'm not saying I don't," Bethany says. "It just makes it easier and less awkward when the time is right, you know? But also, potentially more awkward if your future father-in-law stops by and sits on the couch—which he normally never does—and then finds one under his butt."

Brent groans, covering his face with his hands. "Tell me that didn't happen."

"Oh, it happened. And he got pissed because he wants grandbabies. Can you believe that? I told him he wants more people to torture and he laughed and said he wants to spoil them with obnoxious presents so we're the ones who are tortured."

At the mention of babies, Brent's eyes get really soft and he's staring at Bethany like he wants the impregnating to start right now. I glance between them, half uncomfortable and half jealous, but then Bethany closes her computer with a quick movement and sets it on the table. "Are you ready for ladies' night?" Her voice is too loud. "I got pizza from Bleeker Street!"

"Pizza?" Brent's eyes lighten.

Bethany stands up, coming over to where we're still lingering near the doorway.

"Pizza isn't for you. When are you leaving?" she asks Brent.

Brent crosses his arms over his wide chest. "Do I have to leave? I could be a lady."

Brent is six foot five and two hundred pounds of pure muscle. Despite having heart surgery seven months ago, he's still built like a Greek god. A god of muscles and chiseled good looks.

"Please don't. I love you just the way you are."

"Aw that was sweet and not sarcastic or ridiculous." He frowns at her. "Are you acting opposite of normal because you're being held hostage?" He glances over at me with fake worry.

"Ha ha," Bethany says. "I'm always sweet, dammit. Now get the hell out of here. Your dad is waiting."

"That's the problem," he grumbles, but he doesn't resist when she pushes him toward the door. He leans in to kiss her which makes her growl and push harder. But then she smiles, and they disappear through the doorway for a minute and I'm glad they did because I do not want to see them making out. Hearing it is quite enough for a good thirty seconds while I stew in my own pea-green envy.

"See ya, Scarlett," Brent calls from down the hall and then the door shuts and Bethany reappears.

"Sorry about that," she says. "He's just being cute. Are you hungry? I'm starving."

"I can always eat, unfortunately." I follow her into the kitchen.

She pulls wine glasses down from the cupboard and sets them on the gleaming granite countertop. "What was up with the condom talk with Reese?"

I grimace. "It started because we were talking about Christmas. Her new boyfriend is going to be there."

"Christmas with the family. That's a big deal." She pours wine and then hands me a glass.

I nod. "His parents moved away from Blue Falls, and apparently Granny has taken him in. Along with a few other stragglers from around town for the holidays, and all the rest of the year, I guess."

"Aw that's sweet! Your granny sounds really nice."

I snort. "Sometimes."

"Are you excited to go back home for Christmas? It's been a while, right?"

"Yeah, almost two years." I can't believe I've been away that long. Talking to Reese on the phone is always kind of hard—it makes me homesick and I feel disconnected from her. "Reese sounds so different, older, more mature, I feel like I've missed out on a big part of her life."

Bethany reaches across the counter and pats my hand. "It's important to let people live their lives and grow up—sometimes the best thing you can do is let someone fly on their own."

"Yeah, I know. But sex! She's talking about sex! When she was sixteen, I had to beg her to attend high school. She couldn't talk to boys, let alone consider sleeping with them. It really wasn't that long ago."

"She's how old, nineteen?"

I nod and take a sip of my wine. "Nearly twenty, but I can't help but think of her like a child, still. Or at least childlike. Thankfully they haven't," I lower my voice, "*done it,* yet, but it sounds like it's not for lack of trying on her part."

Bethany's brows lift.

"He wants to wait until she's ready. Well, she's sure she's past ready and onto annoyed, but can't convince him of it."

She grins. "He sounds fun. She should trap him somehow. Maybe kidnap him. Send him on a quest but at the end it's sexy times."

I roll my eyes. "I'll suggest that to her next time we talk." I absolutely won't.

Bethany pulls the pizza out of the oven and we take plates out to the living room.

"How's work going?" I ask when we're seated comfortably on the sofa.

"It's good. Busy, challenging, but I sort of love it. Oh, I meant to tell you about what I found on your Guy."

I almost choke on my pizza. "You mean Guy Chapman? He's not *my* Guy."

She waves a hand in the air. "You know what I mean."

"I do not know what you are referring to."

"Whatever, lady. Listen, I don't care if you want to do the hottie. Lord knows, I've been there. There's no judgment here. I love you no matter who you bang, okay?"

"Got it, but it's not happening."

"Anyway, I was talking to our real estate developer and I guess your Guy has been pretty desperate to get the little lot where you're parking."

"I'm aware."

"Fortunately for you, I already told him not to sell no matter what he offers, but it might get to the point where I can't stop it. He has a backer, Oliver Nichols."

I almost choke on my pizza. "Oliver Nichols the billionaire?"

"Yep."

The delicious pizza turns into a stone ball in my stomach.

"Are they going to have to sell?"

She shrugs. "We're far away from that kind of talk, I wouldn't worry about it. I'll let you know if they keep upping the ante and we reach a point of no return. I'll help you find another place. Or maybe you can buy a brick and mortar; it might be worth it since your catering hustle has been taking off."

"Yeah." I force myself to take a giant bite of pizza even though it's not as delicious as it was a minute ago.

"Did you know he was married?" she asks.

"No. And I don't want to know because it has no relevance." I take a big drink of wine and wait ten full seconds before curiosity gets the best of me. "Okay fine, tell me what you know."

Bethany leans forward, eyes gleaming. "They had a total whirlwind romance, met at a promotional event when he was on that reality TV show. They got married after only a few months, and after less than a month of wedded bliss, it busted up."

"What happened?"

"No one really knows. She disappeared suddenly. This was like a year ago. Now she's all over Instagram, traveling through Europe and stuff. Marie something or other. She's some heiress type but she has a ton of followers because she's like, a lifestyle blogger or some garbage." Bethany shrugs and takes a sip of her wine. "Some people think there was another woman."

"He cheated?"

She waves it off. "I don't think it's true. I also heard he's married to his work, so maybe that's what they meant. Like his work is his mistress. He doesn't have time for a wife, let alone an affair. Plus, his parents are dead and he's raising his sisters."

He mentioned his mom had passed the other night. I wonder what happened. I don't want to feel any sympathy for the brute, but the emotion flickers inside me anyway. "Sisters?"

"Two of them. And one of them has special needs, I guess, so all his time not at the restaurant is with them. So maybe Marie couldn't hang without his undivided attention, she seems like the type. But then again, he was spotted on a date with Maya Roberts only a few weeks after the wife bailed out, so who knows."

"Who's Maya Roberts?"

"Olympic soccer player."

I stew on that and eat more pizza. It doesn't bother me. At all.

"Oh, I know," Bethany snaps and I meet her bright-eyed gaze. "What if he murdered his wife and all the pics on Insta are fakes. That would be, like, the perfect crime. Maybe he buried her in the backyard, hacked into her Insta account and now everyone thinks she's all traipsing the world and poor him but really, he's a total psycho killer."

I can't help but laugh at her enthusiasm. "You think everyone is a murderer."

She sits up straighter. "I do not. I don't think you're capable of cold-blooded killing."

I wait, watching her with raised brows.

She relents. "Well, there is the whole thing where you don't immediately have to yawn when someone else does, and you are totally a scream-sneezer so you might be a sociopath." She eyes me speculatively. "And you're very charming and likeable. Okay, I totally think everyone is a potential murderer."

"It's one of your more irredeemable qualities."

"Fine, no more talk about murder and no more talk about the opposite sex. Tell me what's new in Cupcake-landia. How's Fred?"

We chat about work; I tell her about my big wedding order and all the details involved.

"I don't know how you do it, friend. How are you gonna cater that big an event with just you and Fred?"

"I have the Vulcan which can cook 125 mini cupcakes

in an hour. Then it's a matter of waiting for the cooling and cutting the fondant into the shapes required—that will be the more time-consuming part, but it won't be too hard. I have a plan. I've done large orders before. We'll get it done. I'm not worried."

"I'M STARTING TO WORRY," I tell Fred as I bustle along the sidewalk, hugging my coat tighter. It's getting darker, the sun setting behind the skyscrapers and I swear the temperature has dropped twenty degrees since I left the truck fifteen minutes ago.

"I'm fine."

She sounds like a frog. A sick frog with a plugged nose, harboring a million germs, and this is no good.

I closed up shop early today to get started on the wedding order since Fred won't be able to help me with the fondant toppers. I only have one more batch to throw in the oven and then it's a matter of waiting for them to cool, cutting out the designs, and then getting them into place and into travel containers.

Except all day I've been off. Discombobulated. Mostly due to the fact that I've been working triple time since Fred has been out. I think I've gotten a grand total of five hours of sleep over the last three days. And then this morning, I happened to catch sight of some young blonde getting into Guy's SUV with him. They were gone for an hour and he returned on his own.

Who is she? One of his sisters? I would like to think so, but I doubt it. She appeared too old to be in need of a guardian and Bethany made it sound like they were significantly younger. What bothers me most is I noticed at all and I cared. I shouldn't care. I should hate him.

"Did you go to the doctor?" I ask Fred as I enter the market, bypassing a fake Santa ringing his bell. Christmas music jingles in the background.

"I went yesterday. My flu turned into a pneumonia. I have to take antibiotics for 24 to 48 hours before I stop being contagious. But I should be fine by Monday."

"Don't worry about me. Take care of yourself and come back when you're ready. Did Jack bring you to the doctor?"

"No. He worked late so my mom took me."

I bite my lip from yelling. This is bothersome. He should prioritize Fred.

"You should have called me. I would have gone with you."

"I couldn't do that, you're extra busy since I'm sick. I'm so sorry, Scarlett." She breaks into hacking coughs.

"It's okay, don't worry about me. You worry about resting and getting yourself better."

Mental note to call and have soup delivered since Jack sucks ass.

"I closed up the truck early, and I'm halfway done baking. I need more sugar for the frosting though, so I'm at the store now. Do you need anything? I can grab it and bring it to you on my way back to the truck."

Long pause. "You used all the sugar from the truck?" Her already nasally voice squeaks even higher on the last word.

"Yeah, so?" I bend down to grab a bag of organic sugar from the shelf.

"But…didn't you, I mean, you tasted the first batch, right?"

My gut sinks with sudden intuition. Why would she be asking me this unless . . .? "What? Why are you asking me that?" And why didn't I taste test it? Because I was too busy thinking about Guy's young girlfriend, that's why.

"Oh shit, tell me you didn't! Dammit, Scarlett!" She barks out the words and then breaks into a round of phlegmy coughs.

I drop the bag of sugar and back into someone behind me.

"Excuse me," an acidic voice says, but I barely hear it over the dread filling me.

Fred speaks again. "I told him it wouldn't be a big deal because you always taste the batter on the first batch. And you do! What made you stop now?"

"What do you mean, you told him it was no big deal? What's wrong with my cupcakes?"

"Why didn't you taste test?!"

"I was distracted!"

She blows out a breath and we're both quiet for a few long seconds. "There's salt." Now her voice is small.

"Salt?" It's like I don't even know the meaning of the word.

"You know, the old switch the sugar with salt trick? It's such a lame, predictable prank, how could you have not checked? Who doesn't taste test? You always taste test."

This is it. He's won. He's manipulating my situation to try and get rid of me, just like he manipulates everyone and everything else. I should never have let him rub his face on mine.

"It's my fault, I'm sorry Scarlett. It wasn't him, I—" I hang up. I can't talk to her anymore. I have sixteen hours to bake 1500 more cupcakes and decorate them and yes, I can probably pull it off, but it will mean another all-nighter or nearly an all-nighter and I'm not sure I can take it. If it wasn't for the time it takes for the cooling and the fondant . . .

I'm a failure. I can't cancel or even change an order the day before the wedding, there's no way. All it takes is one bad customer experience for the tales to spread and then no one will hire me, and I'll have to move back to Blue Falls and, and…he'll be right. He can't be right. I can't fail. I have to pull this off. The mother of the bride is going to be enough to ruin me. It's going to be blow torch Scarlett all over again. But worse.

Everything goes silent. I buy the bag of sugar in a daze even though I'll probably need more since I need to re-do the entire order, but none of that is really registering at the moment. I make my way back to the truck, taking a bite to confirm they really are ruined, then a grab a tray of finished, salty product and stalk across the street.

No one notices me striding through the kitchen. Carson is sitting in his little cubby outside Guy's office and I launch a cupcake at his head. He dodges it. "Scarlett, hey!" he calls, but I pass him right by and push open Guy's door.

He's reading some kind of paperwork at his desk and his head lifts at my entrance.

He's utterly unsurprised, expression flat. Even when I start throwing cupcakes at him.

"This." Throw. "Is." Throw "All." Throw. "Your." Throw. "Fault!"

When I'm done, there's mini cupcakes all over his office. Too bad they weren't frosted. As it is, I barely did any damage at all and the lack ratchets up my fury another notch.

"Who is this?" I glance to the side where a man in an elegant three-piece suit is sitting, watching with lifted brows.

"This is Scarlett Jackson," Guy answers him, and my gaze snaps back to his.

"I am also the woman who is going to sue you for... for...existing."

"Now I can see why you've been so reticent," the unknown man says, and the all-consuming anger takes a step back as embarrassment and humiliation move into place.

"Sorry, sir. This doesn't involve you."

He grins. "It likely does, but I'm not sure how much I should admit to. Not while you still have ammunition."

Guy stands. "Oliver, we can talk later. I have something to deal with."

"Clearly." Oliver stands, his gaze roving over me briefly in assessment before he turns to Guy and shakes his hand.

The review wasn't overtly sexual, more evaluating. Not like you would appraise a woman, but like you would examine a particularly interesting specimen of bug or something.

He lifts his brows at Guy and then walks out the door behind me.

Once he's gone, Guy says, "You didn't taste the first batch?"

He would turn this around on me. "That's not the point." I slam my cupcake tray on his desk and a couple of them pop out and roll onto his desk. I've made a little mess of his perfect office and I'm not sad about it.

"How can I fix it?" he asks.

Shocked, I laugh, somewhat manically and pace back and forth in front of his desk. "You want to fix this? You can't. Unless, of course, you want to help me cook 1500 cupcakes and craft detailed fondant tops, in the next 16 hours?"

He blinks. Silence for a few long seconds. Then he gives a short nod. "You've got all the fondant and stencils?"

I nod uncertainly. That didn't put him off at all?

"Right. We can manage it."

He stands, grabbing his coat off the hook. It is a victim of my cupcake drive-by, but he just wipes off some of the cake with a swipe of his hand.

"Carson," he barks.

"Yes, boss." Carson peers around the doorway. Just the top of his head. He's bracing himself for further attack.

"Clean up this mess," Guy tells him. He waves at my feeble attempt at destruction. "And call Clara. Let the girls know I'll be home late and have dinner sent over."

I stand there, watching the exchange in befuddled silence.

"Aye, aye, sir." Carson salutes and gives me a jaunty wink before spinning back to his workstation.

Guy motions for me and leaves out the side door. I follow him, in a complete daze. What is happening? We're standing outside before he speaks.

"What do we need?" he asks.

"Besides twenty-four additional hours in the day?"

"I mean what do we need as far as ingredients."

"Oh. Um. Sugar."

He stops and turns to face me, one brow lifting. "Is that it?"

"I have everything else in the pantry of the truck, but if you have extra mixers, baking trays, and piping bags, that will help."

He nods and talks in a rapid-fire manner I recognize from catching bits of his old show.

"Bring your notes for the order and whatever you have on hand. Go down two doors this way," he points down the length of the building, "I'll get out mixers and sugar and start pre-heating the ovens."

"Right got it."

And then he stalks away, and I have no idea what to do with myself except follow his instructions.

Bustling back to the truck, panicking slightly, I call Bethany. I can't be alone with him for the next…however long this is going to take. I need a buffer.

She answers, "Scarlett!" but sounds breathless and her phone has background noise, like wind. "Where are you?" I ask.

"Hamptons, baby!"

Brent's family has a house there and they occasionally make the trip for the weekend. "Crap."

"Uh oh, what's going on? What's up?"

I give her a quick run-down of everything that's happened in the last hour.

"I'm sorry I can't be there to help but…. So now you're going to use Guy's oven? Using someone's oven sounds like a euphemism for something else."

"Well get your mind out of the gutter because it is not a euphemism for anything but not losing my entire life and reputation and career. Do you think I'm making a mistake?" I ask as I pull the pre-made fondant out of the fridge.

"Depends. Are there other options? You could go to our place and use our oven if you needed to."

"You have a great kitchen, but you only have one oven. He has multiples."

There's a lengthy pause. "Oh. Okay, I get it. He can give you multiples."

I would strangle her if she were in front of me right now. "That's not—"

"No no, it's fine, I'm sure his *appliances* are way better than mine."

I sigh and start rummaging through some of my storage for powdered sugar. "I need help decorating, too, and no number of ovens is going to help me with that. I need hands."

"So, you're saying his hands are good, huh?" She snickers.

"Bethany, I'm not talking about sex, I'm talking about cupcakes!"

"You keep your cupcakes clean, okay? Always make sure the frosting is groomed and the interior is nice and moist."

"You did not just say that word."

She ignores me. "Make sure you use oven mitts, and if he doesn't give you three *blenders*, he's not worth it."

"Bethany, I am not going to have sex with Guy! Ever! It's about cupcakes! I hate you, goodbye!" I push the end button on her laughter right as a throat clears behind me.

Oh, no. I turn around, dread filling me. I know exactly who is at the back door to the truck and who heard me yell, quite loudly, I would not be having sex with him.

"Hi." His mouth is twitching like he's fighting a smile or laughter or some combination of the two and my mortification doubles. "I just came by to see if you needed help carrying anything?"

Chapter Ten

IF YOU WANT TO BECOME A GREAT CHEF, YOU HAVE TO WORK with great chefs.
    —Gordon Ramsay

Guy

"I . . ." She glances around the interior of the truck where she's stacked some ingredients and boxes full of stuff. "I do need help. That would be great."

Her words are fine, but she won't meet my eyes and her face is so bright red it nearly matches her hair. It's adorable.

She turns away, scrambling to throw stuff into one of the boxes and then shoving it at me. "Here. I'll be right there."

I take the box and leave without a word, giving her a chance to collect herself.

Maybe I should be offended that she vehemently denied ever wanting to have sex with me, but while the blow to my ego is more than minimal, I am man enough to understand that I'm not entitled to intimacy from someone just because I crave it.

And she's right. Getting involved with each other would be a terrible idea for so many reasons.

A memory flashes in my mind, when she kissed me at the charity gala, followed immediately by the sensation of her laughing form trapped in my arms during the egg incident. There's something inescapable about her. Alluring. She's all sweet candy and still a little spice. There's the physical attraction, sure, but there's more than that, this sort of mixture of honesty and vulnerability mixed with strength.

I unlock the door to Savor, still awaiting permits but already stocked and outfitted for business, and head back to the storage area to get out the mixers and supplies we might need, setting them out on the counter. My heart thumps a tad wildly in my chest but I don't take the time to examine why the organ is excitable at the thought of spending time with Scarlett.

My phone dings and I pull it from my pocket. There's a text from Oliver.

LET me know if you want help with the Marie situation.

SOMEHOW WHEN HE was over earlier, my divorce—or lack thereof—had come up. Oliver hinted strongly that he could help push things along. How? I'm not entirely sure. I think the man has blackmail material on everyone in town and then some. I don't want to be beholden to him more than I already am, though, so I told him thanks but no thanks.

The door swings open and I forget all about Oliver and Marie and possibly my own name as Scarlett walks into the kitchen, her hair a messy bun on her head, her face bare of makeup. She's fresh and sweet, and nothing at all like the fiery amazon that launched cupcakes at my head just short while ago.

She glances around uncertainly. "Where should I . . .?" She holds up the box.

"Here." Stalking in her direction, I take it. "You can put your coat in one of the cubbies over there." I motion to the open doorway by the entrance, an alcove for employees to leave their personal items.

I wash my hands while she hangs up her coat and puts on an apron, not because my hands are dirty but because I need to do something other than ogle her.

She walks over to where I set the box and starts pulling items out.

I stop beside her. "I got out some things that might help." I point out the mixers, bowls, and other accoutrements. "Now tell me what to do."

"We'll need to bake and cool, but the most time-consuming part will be decorating. The theme is Beatles, so I'm doing little Beatle heads for the fondant decoration."

I stare at her, surprised and confused. "Beetle…heads?"

A slow smile spreads across her face. "Sorry, not beetles. The Beatles. Like John, Paul, George and Ringo, not the black bugs with twitchy claw hands."

"Thank God for that."

She smiles and looks down at the list in her hand. "There are stencils for their heads—outlines of hair and mustaches, basically, and a guitar stencil. I premade and sealed the fondant."

"Okay."

"Here's the order details and recipe lists. There are four different flavors with six different fondant tops." She hands it to me and our fingers brush, making my heart stutter in my chest for a moment. "We'll need to make extra of each, just in case."

"Of course." I focus on the list in my hand, scanning down the ingredients and details, my eyes halting at a surprising ingredient.

"Sour cream?"

She nods.

"That's why they're so moist."

She flushes and her eyes dart away, clearing her throat around a laugh. "Um. Yeah. An old trick my granny taught me."

I keep reading. "This is a pretty intense order."

"Yeah." She bites her lip. "They're spending a pretty penny, so I gotta get everything right. It's a sweet story, actually. They met in Strawberry Fields."

"In Central Park?"

She nods. It's a memorial, a couple acres of real estate directly across from the Dakota Apartments where John Lennon lived and died.

"They are both big fans."

"Well, with wedding flavors like Rocky Road Raccoon, Sexy Cinnamon Sadie, and Hey Jude Peppermint Java, I would hope so."

She grins suddenly, the movement lighting up her whole face. "I came up with the names, you like them?"

An answering smile tugs at my mouth. "I do."

We stare at each other for a few long seconds and then her smile falters.

"Right. Let's get going. Time waits for no woman in need of cake."

We organize the ingredients and move around the kitchen, getting the batter made quickly with the mixers and loading the trays once they are done.

I've cooked with a lot of chefs, both experts and aspiring, but I'm not sure I've ever made cupcakes with one. And it's not as awkward as I had thought. We move around each other with surprising ease, exchanging bags of flour, cartons of eggs, and both of us double-checking the sugar before dumping it into the mixers.

Once things are baking, we work on the fondant tops, standing next to each other, each of us pressing out a roll on the counter to get it stretched and pliant.

"I'm sorry about the salt thing," I say.

She glances over at me, stopping her rolling efforts to stare, her pink mouth popped open in surprise.

"Fred helped me, but it's my fault. It was my idea. And I wouldn't have done it if I had known you wouldn't taste the first batch."

She shrugs. "It's okay. I normally taste test, but I

was…distracted, I guess. And you're making up for it now."

We get caught in each other's gaze again but this time I yank my eyes away, rolling out my fondant with renewed vigor.

She hands me some of the stencils and I get to work cutting and tracing with a precision cutter while she continues rolling out some black fondant.

"So, when are you opening the rest of this building?"

"There's still some construction here in the dining area, you probably noticed on your way in. But it should be opened by the end of the month. It's going to be a whole experience for diners, from the sweet to the savory."

She bites her lip and I squash down the tension filling my gut. I don't like that she's uneasy about our situation, even though it shouldn't bother me. It's business. That's it. But still. Maybe I should use this opportunity to needle her and make her even more uncomfortable. But I can't. Instead, I change the subject.

"What made you decide to start a food truck?"

She clears her throat and focuses on stenciling shapes from her black fondant. I watch her work, appreciating her form and her toned arms. Not really surprising considering her job. Her movements are surprisingly efficient. *She's* surprisingly efficient. Except for the flour on her shoulder. "Well, mostly I was having trouble finding a job at a real restaurant because I set a pretty influential chef on fire."

I rub the back of my neck in chagrin. "And he told everyone? What a dick."

She bursts out laughing and I feel a thousand times better.

"It was a lot harder than I thought it would be. There's a lack of available space, you know."

"I hadn't heard," I say drily.

She smiles. "It's more than that, though. The permit process is a nightmare. Did you know they only give out a certain number, a little over 4,000, and they haven't adjusted the available amount since 1980. So, there's a huge waiting list. You may not have to wait though, if you're willing to spend $20,000.00 to get a black-market permit. On top of that, there are excessive regulations for where and when you can park, and you have to follow all the appropriate health code regulations, which means being inspected and storing everything in a commissary overnight."

The timers go off and we remove the tins and set them out to cool, putting in another batch while we continue to work on the tops.

Through all of this, part of my mind stews over our situation. If only there was a way to tie in her food truck with the rest of the block…. But no. It would never work. The theme is completely off, and Oliver will never agree. He's a pragmatic when it comes to details, and yet surprisingly superstitious. If it's not effortless, he thinks it's a sign that it's not meant to be. For a brilliant rich guy, he's also somewhat absurd.

The cakes cool and we continue to work together, piping frosting onto each small cake and meticulously pressing the fondant tops on hundreds and hundreds of times over. Time passes in a whir of activity, and then suddenly—we're done.

She watches me set the final cupcake into the plastic clamshell container, ready to be transported to....

"Where's the wedding at?" I ask her.

"Bay Room."

"I'll have these shipped over in the morning so they can be there for you to set up the display whenever you need to." I turn to face her. She's leaning one side against the counter and I mimic her stance.

"Are you sure?" There's a crease between her brows and gray smudges underneath her eyes. She's got to be exhausted.

My eyes wander over her features. She has a little bit of white frosting stuck to the side of her bottom lip. "You can trust me. I wouldn't turn this into a prank, not after all that work."

I glance over at the clock. It's a bit after midnight. Not too shabby.

"I believe you, it's just.... Why are you helping me?" She steps closer.

I shrug. "It was my fault, which makes it my responsibility to make it right."

"But it really doesn't. And we're at war, remember?"

Without thought, I move toward her, tracing my thumb over the generous bow of her bottom lip to remove the frosting. I bring my thumb to my mouth, sucking the sweet topping and gauging her reaction.

Her mouth pops open. Her eyes dilate, and an answering pulse responds throughout my entire body.

And just like that, everything inside me spills over, like a pot of boiling water left on high.

The strength of my own need is a shock to the core. It's ridiculous. Improbable and completely self-indulgent. We're completely wrong for each other.

And yet the memory of our first and last kiss hits me like a cast iron pan to the head. That wasn't a fluke. Her scent overwhelms me, warm vanilla and sugar and I'm starving for it.

My body takes over my brain and I can only watch as my hands reach out and slide into her hair. I rest my thumbs on her cheeks, feeling the heat of her. I want it.

She doesn't stop me, doesn't pull away, even though I keep my hold light enough that all she has to do is move back.

But she doesn't.

Instead, she moves into me and tilts up, bringing herself so close, a mere inch is all that's needed to bring our mouths together.

When her tongue slides against mine, I lift her onto the prep table. She spreads her legs easily and I step between them. Her hands are greedy little beggars, pulling my shirt from my pants and skipping up my back, exploring the tension, rubbing my spine like I'm a cat.

I groan and she gasps and then my hands are insatiable, untying her apron at her back so I can glide my fingers up the soft flesh of her stomach and up farther, cupping her breasts with light palms over her bra.

Her mouth leaves mine for a moment, but only so she can pull the apron off and then she's unbuttoning her shirt with trembling fingers. I try to help her, but I can't focus on anything but the creamy skin she's exposing, and a sheer lavender bra that does little to hide her curves and shape.

With a moan, I sink in and suck at her breasts over her bra. She goes a little wild, holding my head in place while simultaneously trying to press our hips closer.

"Guy." My name is a plea and the sensation of her cloth-covered nipple, hard in my mouth, along with her hips struggling for mine is almost too much. I'm no longer an experienced man, I'm back to being a teenage virgin.

And then my phone dings with incoming texts, three times in rapid succession.

The sound is like an alarm going off in both our heads. She rears back, her breathing erratic, and I release my hold, walking over to where I left my phone to check the message.

It's a string of texts from Emma, mostly random emojis and one blurry picture of the side of her face. For someone with a nerve disorder who struggles to walk and even reach for things sometimes, the girl sure knows how to use a cell phone and iPad. Her timing is impeccable. She texts me mostly, and Oliver. At first, I was surprised they were communicating. Not that he's a bad guy, or anything, you'd just think a billionaire would have better things to do with his time. But he's always been one of the few people in my life who enjoys spending time with the girls and Emma gets a kick out of all the goat gifs he sends her.

I put the phone aside and stare at Scarlett across the room.

She's staring at me, dazed, lips swollen. I did that. A

surge of macho satisfaction sweeps through me and I walk back over to her, ready to pick up where we left off, but she glances around, as if just now realizing her position and yanks her legs and shirt together.

"I'm sorry," she says. Her cheeks tinge pink.

My hands reach for her, but I force them down, clenching my fists at my sides. "You have nothing to be sorry for."

"It's just…this is . . . ." One hand lifts and then drops in ineffectual gesturing.

"I know, I know." I step back further. "I'm a butt-sniffing turd nugget."

She bursts out a laugh and a smile tugs at my lips. I can't believe I can smile at all, considering most of my focus and blood flow is contained on my aching erection. Watching her laugh, unrestrained, her clothes a total mess, and yet still as beautiful as the most imperfect and enticing thing in the world isn't helping the problem.

"It's not that. This is a bad idea."

Something in my chest aches. A bad idea? Not to me. Not at the current moment. As a matter of fact, touching her is the best idea I can think of, but I can't tell her that. Not without her giving her the upper hand. And even though what she's saying is exactly what I was thinking myself, hearing the words still stings.

"Is it a bad idea, though?" I throw it out there like it's a joke.

She watches me carefully and then her eyes lower. "Besides the whole trying to commandeer my spot— which is enough on its own—I've dated chefs before. It never ends well."

I should let it go. She's right. I can't be with someone I'm actively trying to…get rid of—and I mean that in the least murderous way possible. And still, I can't stop the words. "Maybe you were just with the wrong chefs."

She's already shaking her head in denial. Not meeting my eyes, buttoning her shirt up with hands that tremble slightly. I want to reach for her, hold her, but I can't.

"It wasn't just chefs. And it's not only them. It's me. I am too trusting. Too willing to love and ignore and let people manipulate me into believing they cared. Every boyfriend I ever had either cheated, lied, or both. My last serious relationship ended up being married. Hell, even when I first moved here and tried to date around like a normal person, someone tried to drug me. I'm just… never quite enough."

"So, you've given up on relationships entirely? That doesn't seem like you." Scarlett is stubborn. That I know for a fact. And I don't know exactly what it is, whether it's the baking, the sweetness and honesty, or the playful happiness she exudes like a fragrance, but Scarlett is like a comfortable blanket. A sexy, alluring, comfortable blanket. She deserves love and romance and everything, if that's what she wants.

"You don't know me."

She's right, I don't really know her. Another part of her little speech chews on me. Technically, I'm also a married man, but that's different. It's on paper only. I would be divorced by now if Marie wasn't trying to delay the inevitable for as long as possible. But I don't tell Scarlett. I doubt she would care either way considering we aren't even dating.

More concerning to me is her self-deprecatory remarks. "Your past experiences…. Those have nothing to do with you and everything to do with them being assholes."

And then I catch myself and the words register. I am an asshole. I have been, in her eyes and apparently everyone else. I nod. "Point proven."

She's shaking her head, reaching out a hand then dropping it to her side. "Wait, Guy, you're not—"

"I hold no false illusions about myself. I know I can be…heartless."

"Sometimes. But you're human. And you're not an asshole all the time, otherwise you wouldn't have helped me tonight when you didn't have to."

"No. You were right before, I am. This changes nothing."

She doesn't get upset; she considers me, head half-cocked, and she smiles. The move is so angelic, sweet, with a hint of vixen. "I guess we're still sworn enemies, then."

"I guess so."

"Sworn enemies who sometimes make out." She winces and her brows pull together in concern. "Is that normal?"

"Not that I'm aware of."

"You don't do this with all your arch nemeses?"

"No."

We exchange a glance, the air full of pent-up lust and regret, fighting it out between us.

"I better put everything away," I say.

"I'll help," she says.

"Will you need help tomorrow with the set up?"

Her brows lift in surprise, and then she shakes her head. "No. Thank you, though. It's probably best if we keep our distance."

I turn away, grabbing some dirty pans to put in the sink. "You're right."

We clean up in silence, the void between us growing.

Chapter Eleven

EATING IS SO INTIMATE. IT'S VERY SENSUAL. WHEN YOU invite someone to sit at your table and you want to cook for them, you're inviting a person into your life.

    —Maya Angelou

Scarlett

IT'S ALMOST A SUPERPOWER—THE ability to experience everything that can go wrong in the shortest amount of time possible.

The train wasn't on time because of signal delays—which is something that happens all the time. I should have left earlier and been more prepared, but I wasn't because I was too busy daydreaming about Guy's mouth and hands and tongue and body parts in general.

The wedding is at the Bay Room in the Financial District—an imposing building named The Liberty

Skyscraper. The room itself is on the 60th floor, and its full name is actually, "The Bay Room at Manhatta", with no N, like it's too pretentious to carry the extra letter.

It took me forever to get up to the 60th floor and then I had to fight with an attendant to get in because he didn't think I belonged. I'm wearing one of my nicest dresses, a deep purple with a square neckline and flared skirt. He's not wrong, exactly, but I couldn't bail because my appearance is more Bridge and Tunnel than Upper East Side. Finally, the wedding planner saw me and yelled at the attendant and hustled me back to the kitchen.

Except I couldn't find the cupcakes. At first, I thought Guy had totally duped me and didn't have them delivered, but then why go through all the trouble of helping me make them if he was going to con me? And then one of the kitchen staff remembered seeing them earlier that morning. Finally, we found them, stuffed into the back of a giant walk in fridge. But by then, I was running out of time.

I'm flustered. Panicking. I can't even get the cakes onto the tiered stand because I'm rushing too much, and I've dropped three already. Presentation is just as important as taste. This has to be perfect.

I'm in the corner of the kitchen while the catering staff bustles around behind me, yelling and talking and clanking dishes.

I can do this.

"You have ten minutes," the wedding planner says as she rushes past me, holding a giant arrangement of calla lilies.

"I'm on it." I take a few deep breaths. I can do this.

I place the mini cakes steadily and carefully, and then there's a voice behind me.

"Scarlett, darling, that color is fabulous on you."

I spin around and Carson is there, air kissing me on both cheeks. "I could eat you like one of your cupcakes."

I grip his upper arms and scan him like he's an apparition. "Carson? What are you doing here?"

It's like he, poof, magically appeared in front of me in a suit. Like a fairy godmother, except with a mustache.

"A little birdie told me you might need some help. Except, it wasn't a bird, it was a cantankerous chef who is clearly smitten with you."

My face heats. He doesn't know about the make-out session. Sessions. Plural. He can't. Guy wouldn't tell him.

"He is not smitten with me."

"Okay, you keep telling yourself that, princess. But he let you use a new kitchen. It might as well be a declaration of his intentions. He sent me and I'm being paid, so tell me how I can help?"

I'm too happy he's here to spend any time complaining, so I show him the cakes, the tiers, and the decorations I brought, little Beatle bobbleheads, mini guitar figurines, a yellow submarine, British style telephone booth, and mini British flags.

Carson is efficient and bright, setting the adornments around the cakes strategically and making suggestions as we place the decorative items so it's quirky and cute instead of completely haphazard.

My fingers place the mini cupcakes on the tiers, but my mind is spinning.

He did this. He sent Carson because he wanted to

help but didn't want to disrespect my wish to keep our distance. And like the contradictory fool I am, suddenly I want to see him. Stupidly, I wish he had ignored my request and come instead of Carson, but then that would make him a pushy jerk and I wouldn't be wanting to see him, most likely. How dare he?

We have a majority of the cakes set up lickety-split and I finally take a breath.

Carson helps me roll the table out to the reception area and lock the wheels and then we can leave. I always make extra, just in case there's any mishaps, so I give Carson a box to take home. I still have a dozen in one of my transportable containers.

Normally, I love staying to watch the bride and groom interact on their wedding day. It gives me hope that someday I might find something real, but tonight Carson and I head back down to the ground floor in the elevator together.

"What are you up to now?" I ask him.

"Meeting my boyfriend for dinner. You want to come?"

"No, it's fine." The thirdest of all wheels. That's me.

"Where are you headed? Maybe we could share a cab?" he offers.

"Maybe . . ." But I don't want to go home. My stomach is stirring with something. Butterflies. I shouldn't, but it's like I can't help it. Need swirls through me. Need to see him. I clench the cupcake container in my hands. And I have the perfect excuse for stopping by. "Do you know where Guy is right now?" I ask.

Carson quirks a brow at me. "At home, probably."

"Will you give me his address?"

His mouth opens in mock horror. "How dare you! I would never betray him in such a fashion and tell you his apartment is on 81st street in the Upper East Side. And he totally does not go to the pool this time of night with his sisters. And if he's not there he will not be in apartment number 1070. And I will not go in with you so the concierge lets you in since he knows me and owes me a personal favor for making sure Guy tips extra every Christmas."

"Thanks Carson, I won't tell him you didn't tell me. Or something."

"Something tells me he's going to be happy I didn't," he says with a smirk.

GUY'S APARTMENT building is exactly what I would choose, if I had the funds to do so. It's in one of the best neighborhoods, with great security and a concierge in the front lobby. It's one of those places with multiple room accommodations, and yes, even a pool on the ground floor —a not insignificant feat in a city where it's hard to even find a parking spot for a Fiat.

After we check in with the concierge, I follow Carson to the pool room, but before we go in, he stops outside the steamy doors. The sound of splashing and laughter trickle out into the hall. "He's in there with his sisters."

"You're not coming in with me?"

"I don't think he'll want to see me."

"But he'll want me here?" My voice squeaks out.

Carson nods. "And I gotta meet Mark in," he glances at his watch, "ten minutes."

"You don't think he'll be mad?" This seemed like such a good idea until I saw the building but now the urge to run is flipping through me like a gymnast doing cartwheels in my belly.

Carson shrugs, unconcerned. "I doubt it. If he asks, though, I was never here." He hugs me quickly and then runs away.

Damn him.

I'm so tempted to leave, but equally tempted to see him and…what? Make out with him? Or just thank him. I glance down at the plastic container in my hand. I've got it. If it's weird, I will give him and his sisters some cakes and leave. I can manage that.

Bolstered, I straighten my shoulders and push into the chlorine-scented room.

The room is warm and steamy and huge. Scattered strategically around the sides are palm fronds, and around the pool, loungers, chairs, and tables. Brightness glows overhead, some kind of built-in lighting that mimics actual sunlight.

Then I focus on the people in the room.

Guy is sitting on the edge, his feet in the water. Two dark heads bob in the center of the pool. They appear to be about the same size, but one is wearing blow up arm bands and has a pink flamingo circular floating device around her waist.

"You have ten more minutes," Guy calls out.

"Fifteen," a young voice calls back.

"Eight."

"That's not fair!"

The girl in the flamingo inflatable splashes at Guy, then proceeds to laugh loudly when the spray hits him.

"Seven," he says, but there's laughter in his voice, too.

He's relaxed and happy and the banter between them makes my heart twist in my chest. It's one thing to hear he's raising his sisters; to witness it in person adds a whole new layer of awareness to the situation. This man is not what he presents to the rest of the world. Not at all.

The girl in the pool spins and kicks herself away, and the other girl, the one without any inflatables, turns and sees me.

"That's a pretty dress," she says.

"Thanks." I glance down and then up in time to see Guy twisting to see me.

"Scarlett." His eyes are bright in the artificial lights. "What are you doing here?" His words are clipped with surprise.

"I, uh, wanted to bring you these." I hold up the cupcake container. "As a little thank you. But I don't mean to interrupt. I'll leave them here and—"

"Are those for us?" His sister asks. She's holding on to the side of the pool, watching me with clear interest. The other girl in the pink tube tries to clutch at the side, too, but her inflatable keeps getting in the way and water splashes over the side. She bounces more, spilling more water outside the pool and laughing with glee.

"Yes, if your, uh, brother says it's okay." I set them on a nearby table and wave awkwardly. "I'll be going then."

"Wait." His voice stops me.

"We were about to go up to eat dinner. Would you like to join us?"

Now it's my turn to be surprised. He's inviting me to dinner? With his sisters?

The disbelief momentarily stole my tongue, and suddenly he's the one rambling. "It's okay if you have other plans, I thought since you're here already and you brought dessert and—"

"Yes." I cut him off with a short bark of a reply and then collect myself. "Yes, I would love to stay for dinner, thank you for the invitation."

"Do you want to come swimming?" One of his sisters asks me.

"I'm afraid I'm rather unprepared, but maybe some other time," I say.

Her head tilts. "You can put your feet in, if you want."

My gaze locks with Guy's. He pats the concrete next to him and I nod, a smile tugging at the corners of my lips. I take off my heels and leave them next to the table where I put the cupcakes. Then I walk over to Guy and sit down a foot away from him, slipping my feet into the luke-warm water.

"What's your name?" his sister asks, still clutching the side of the pool.

Guy speaks before I can respond. "Sorry, I should have introduced you. These are my sisters, Ava and Emma." He points out Ava, the talker, and Emma, the one in the pink flamingo tube, bouncing up and down slightly and making the water wave. "Girls, this is Scarlett. She's, uh . . ."

"We're friends." I help him out so he doesn't feel

obligated to try and explain our relationship to his sisters. "I'm a chef, too."

"Do you make fancy food like Guy does?" Ava asks.

"Not quite."

"Well, that's good because his food is gross. Hey, maybe she should make us dinner."

I laugh. Only a kid would think a Michelin-rated chef makes "gross" food.

"You think mac and cheese from a box with fake cheddar is better than my gruyere and poblano white cheddar mac and cheese."

She wrinkles her nose. "It even sounds disgusting."

Emma laughs the sound both rough and uninhibited, and then she splashes jerkily at her sister. "Okay, okay, I'm coming. She likes it when I pull her," Ava tells me as she sweeps her away and they swim down the side of the pool.

"How long have they lived with you?" I ask Guy.

"Since before our dad died…. It's been about five years now. They're twins."

"How old are they?"

"They turned thirteen last month."

Water splatters across my face and down the front of my dress and I squeak in surprise.

"She's really sorry," Ava rushes to explain. "She likes you but she can't say it any other way."

"It's fine." I laugh and wipe some water off my face with my hand. "It's just water."

Guy and Ava are watching me intently, like they expect me to freak out or something, and it makes me giggle a little nervously. "Really, it's fine. You just wanted me to get the full experience of the pool, right?" I say to

Emma. She doesn't meet my eyes, instead watching her hands flap in the water.

Ava smiles at me, a small tilt of lips, and then pulls Emma away to the other side of the pool.

"Emma has Angelman Syndrome," Guy says.

"What does that mean?"

He rubs the back of his head. "In scientific terms, it's a chromosomal disorder. Deletion or defect on chromosome 15. It's pretty rare. The range of how people are affected by it varies by subtype. Emma has no maternal 15. She can't speak, but she does understand what we're saying. She communicates mostly through gestures, and things like facial movements. She has an iPad she really likes, and she texts me a lot. Mostly emojis and pictures. She's been getting into videos lately, too."

I nod. Not really sure how to react, or even how much I can understand. Sorry doesn't seem right, there's nothing *wrong* with Emma.

"Why did you...why did you really come here?" he asks.

"I wanted to tell you thank you, for sending Carson."

"You could have told me tomorrow."

"I...I have no real excuse." I go for brutal honesty. "I know what I said before about how we should keep our distance but...I wanted to see you."

Eyes lock. My heart is pounding. What am I doing? This is crazy. And stupid. We both decided this was a bad idea. He's still going to try and make me move, and I'm still going to fight him tooth and nail. So why am I here? What am I expecting this to lead to? Except heart break for me. And yet, we keep having these sorts of magical moments together, and I'm not just referring to the sexual variety.

"I told your sister I am your friend. Maybe that could be the truth." I stare at my toes in the water, watching the rippling waves so I don't have to meet his eyes.

"No," he says.

"No?" My heart is sinking. This was a bad idea. This isn't a magical moment.

"I'm not sure I could ever be just friends with you."

My sinking heart lifts and stutters into a double time beat. "What—?"

"We're hungry," Ava calls from the other side of the pool. Emma is clutching her hand as they exit via the steps on the other side.

Guy jumps up and walks briskly to the girls, helping Emma out of her floatation devices and handing out towels, wrapping one around Emma's shoulders.

Watching him interact with them is like examining an alien species. He's still the same--serious, intense, completely focused on their needs, but there's an under-lying level of care.

His focus shifts and his eyes meet mine from across the pool.

"Dinner and cupcakes?"

I pull my legs out of the water. "I'm in."

Chapter Twelve

A GOOD CHEF HAS TO BE A MANAGER, A BUSINESSMAN AND A great cook. To marry all three together is sometimes difficult.
 –Wolfgang Puck

Guy

WHEN I FIRST SAW SCARLETT STANDING IN the pool room with wide eyes and a blank expression, my heart almost stopped. Not because I didn't want to see her, but because the last time I introduced a woman to my sisters, it didn't end well. I don't think Scarlett is anything like Marie, but I didn't realize Marie was like Marie until it was too late, and the memory still lingers like the smell of burnt toast.

But when she asked questions and listened without comment or judgment, didn't freak out when her dress got wet, and then even talked to Emma like anyone else...that meant something.

We make our way upstairs, walking behind Ava who is holding onto Emma's hand to help her walk to the elevator. Emma's movements are jerky and somewhat unsteady.

"Did you bring chocolate cupcakes?" Ava asks Scarlett.

"Of course."

Ava's smile is bright, tossed over her shoulder and flashed in our direction like a sunbeam. "Good."

A pang flares in the vicinity of my chest. It's my fault Ava is so wary of strange women I bring into our lives. Ava is very protective of Emma, like her little personal bodyguard.

Once we're in the apartment, I lead Scarlett to the living room and then tell the girls to go shower.

"Do you need help with the food?" Scarlett asks.

I'm picking up discarded items strewn about the room, sweaters, old food containers, coloring books and pens. "No, it's fine."

I glance over at her, standing in my living room and wonder what she thinks of the space.

It's a rather luxurious building, maybe an unnecessary expense, but I wanted something nice for the girls with a pool to use as therapy for Emma. Not to mention the fact that she loves the water, which is hard enough to find in New York City. But living with two teen girls, one of whom has special needs, isn't conducive to opulent living. The space is open and functional, with comfortable dark couches and swept hard wood. Since Emma isn't stable on her feet, there's no hard corners or anything she could trip on. But there is a bright green stain on the rug from when Ava dropped some sensory goop, and I've never quite been able to get the glitter out of the arm of the reclining chair.

The Christmas tree in the corner is not one of those tastefully decorated ensembles that could come out of a department store. Nope. I let the girls decorate, which means Ava tried to make the ornaments somewhat uniform while Emma delights in lumping them all in the same corner. Most of our ornaments are handmade art projects from both girls, but mostly Emma. She loves art and making things with her hands, despite, or perhaps because of, the unsteadiness of her fine motor skills.

"I can boil water like a pro. Or at least supervise." She's smiling at me and a little bit of tension slips from my shoulders.

"Okay."

In the kitchen, she leans against the counter as I pull out the pot and fill it with water.

"Are we having fancy mac and cheese for dinner?" she asks.

"No. Nothing fancy, some spaghetti Bolognese. The sauce is in the Crock Pot. You want to stir it?"

She nods and moves over to the small appliance, picking up the wooden spoon set in a spoon rest and lifts the lid. "You use a Crock Pot?"

I shrug. "Anything that will make life easier. It's functional for things you need to keep on a simmer. That surprises you?"

"I didn't picture you as the type."

"What type?"

"I don't know. I guess I think of people who use Crock Pots as soccer moms and people who use Pinterest." She stirs the sauce. "It smells good."

"You think I'm too snobby to condescend to using a Crock Pot?" I stand right next to her, putting the pot on the oven and clicking the heat on.

"Maybe. Maybe I thought that before." She puts the cover back over the sauce and turns to face me. We're only a foot apart, close enough to touch.

"Not anymore?"

She smiles. "No."

"Scarlett, do you like Mr. Bean?" Ava calls from the living room.

Her brows lift. "Mr. Bean?" she asks me.

"It's one of Emma's favorites."

"I'm sure I'll love it."

She disappears into the living room and I gaze blankly at the stove, listening to Scarlett ask Ava more questions about Mr. Bean while Emma makes happy sounds as she participates in the conversation in her own way.

I dump the noodles in and then peek into the living room to check out the situation.

Scarlett is on the couch in the middle—my normal spot—with Ava on one side and Emma on the other. Emma shows her something on the tablet.

"Seven minutes," I tell them.

"Good, I'm starving," Ava moans.

Ten minutes later we're sitting at the table in the dining room.

"This is really good." Scarlett chews up a small bite. "Prego or Ragu?"

I widen my eyes at her. "How dare you?"

We laugh and Emma laughs too, a picture of unrestrained joy.

Scarlett smiles. "You have the best laugh, Emma."

"I think so, too," Ava says. "People at my school, they think it's weird." She wrinkles her nose.

"Their loss," I say.

Ava shrugs and pats her sister on the shoulder. "Emma, you're the best sister in the world."

Emma reaches for Ava, too, her hand patting her on the back with jerky movements and leaving spaghetti stains on her shirt.

"When we went to Disney World last year, we didn't even have to wait in lines," Ava brags.

"That's a bonus."

"But people stare sometimes. I don't like it."

"They are probably curious," Scarlett says.

Ava shrugs. "I guess. Can we have cupcakes now?"

I nod. "Fine. But tell Scarlett thank you for bringing them."

Ava and Emma both scramble from the table to put their plates in the sink. "Thank you, Scarlett!" Ava calls as they're running away.

They eat cupcakes and we finish our wine and watch one episode of Mr. Bean in the living room before it's time for the kids to go to bed.

I leave Scarlett by herself in the living room so Ava and I can help Emma get ready for bed and brush her teeth. Emma is energetic, probably a mixture of sugar and having a new person in our apartment making her excitable. She keeps trying to put her toothbrush in my mouth and laughing.

Eventually, the girls are in the room they share and under the covers.

I kiss them both goodnight and cut off the light, shutting their door behind me.

Back in the living room, I find Scarlett standing by one of the shelves, holding a photo of me and the girls at the Museum of Natural History, a giant whale sculpture behind us.

"This is cute," Scarlett holds it up.

"They love animals." I walk over to where she's standing, stopping when I get about a foot away.

She smiles at me and sets the photo back on the shelf. "They're really great."

"I think so."

She faces me again and considers me in silence. "You're like two different people."

I shake my head. "Not really."

"I can't reconcile this version of you—the family man —with the professional perfectionist who demands the same of everyone and would never let anyone stand in the way of his goals."

I take a small breath in and give her the unadulterated truth. "I can't control a lot of things in my life. So, I take care of what I can. It's not so much letting people get in the way of my goals, it's more that I would never let anyone stand in the way of me doing my best for my family. They've been through enough."

She nods slowly. "I get it." She glances around the living room. "I should probably get going."

"One more glass of wine?" I wonder if she can hear the thick thread of hope in the words.

Maybe she can, because she searches my eyes for a few seconds and then nods. "One more."

I pour her a glass of wine and then check on the girls to make sure they're actually sleeping before coming back to the living room.

We sit on the couch, Mr. Bean still playing softly in the background, the flickering of the TV casting shadows and light over her face.

"They share a room?" she asks.

"Yes. Emma doesn't sleep well. Insomnia is a common problem in children with Angelman's. She wakes up at 3 a.m. at least once a week. Ava insists on being there if Emma needs her."

"That's so sweet."

I nod. "She's great, but I also worry for her."

"Why?"

"Emma will require care for the rest of her life. Ava insists that since they shared a womb, she wants to be the one to do it. Demands it, really. She says she was there in the beginning and she'll be there until the end. But I worry it's not fair to her. I don't want her to feel obligated, I guess. Or like she can't go off to college and experience life on her own."

Scarlett smiles. "They are both pretty amazing. Emma, when she laughs, it's like...listening to happiness in its most authentic form."

I want to reach out and touch her, but instead I pick up my wine glass. "I get what you mean. She's definitely taught me a lot about life and love. Especially since our parents died."

"What happened to them? If you don't mind me asking."

"It's fine." I take a sip of wine before answering. "Our mom died first. She had pancreatic cancer. By the time she was diagnosed, it was too late to do surgery or treat it with anything but hospice and end of life care. Just things to make her as comfortable as possible. Dad took care of her, non-stop. Wouldn't leave her side, so that's when I took the girls in. After mom died, dad wasn't far behind. He got sick. A flu bug that turned into pneumonia, and he just kind of gave up."

"I'm sorry." She puts a hand on my arm, and I stare down at it. She has small hands, nails clipped short, and painted a vivid hot pink. They are bright and happy, just like she is.

I meet her eyes. "Thank you. Mom had Emma and Ava when she was older. Twins were a surprise. They're twenty years younger than I am."

Her eyes are luminous in the dim light and I don't want to talk about anything that won't put a smile on her face. "I'm sorry. This is a really depressing conversation."

"It isn't. And I asked. Death is a part of life."

"That's true, but I'm talking about myself too much. Tell me about your family. Your parents…they're sort of famous."

She sighs and shifts a little on the couch. Her hand leaves my arm to reach for the wine glass on the side table, and I miss the gentle pressure.

"Ah, yes," she says.

"I may have done some light stalking," I admit.

She gives me the side eye before taking a sip of the wine. "You don't say."

"Are you close with them?"

"Ha!"

"I guess that's a no?"

She swirls the wine glass in her hand and turns a little to face me, resting her elbow on the back of the sofa. ""Jasper and Violet Jackson. Famed artists and creative geniuses," she intones with a sigh. "I never see them. You know they're gonna be here at some fancy show in Harlem, and they didn't even tell me? My Granny told me. She says I should go see them, but . . ."

"You don't want to?"

She shrugs. "If I want to be ignored by my parents, I can do that from the privacy of my own home in my jammies, no need to be shamed in public."

"They wouldn't ignore you, would they?"

"Eh, they might make an effort for a few minutes then they would get distracted by someone more exciting. They weren't exactly enthused that Reese and I aren't artistically inclined, and if you aren't in their sphere then you're no one."

"Cooking is an art."

"I think so, too, but they don't see it that way. Food to them is only a means of obtaining energy to create something the world at large can be impressed by."

"Is your sister artistically inclined?"

"No. Not at all. She's a total brainiac in like everything but art. She's in college now, earning a double major in physics and math with a minor in business."

"Wow. That's impressive."

Scarlett smiles, glowing with pride. "She's the best. But she's always been inherently shy, not a fan of the spotlight, and the complete opposite of my parents. Thankfully. With Reese, I didn't feel alone as a kid, even though we're six years apart in age. I miss her a lot. I felt bad leaving her in Texas…but."

"You had to get away from the ex?"

"Yeah. That and I didn't want to be the reason Reese didn't fly the nest. She needed a little nudge. As for the ex…he didn't think I would make it here. In fact, he told me I would be back within six months."

Should I tell her Marie and I are still technically married? I immediately squash the notion.

No. It doesn't matter. We're as good as done and it's not like I'm thinking about remarrying any time soon. Talk of my ex would definitely ruin the moment. So instead I say, "You showed him."

"So far."

I nod.

We're quiet for a few long seconds, understanding the implications behind her words but refusing to address them.

She takes a sip of wine and sets the glass down on the coffee table. When she sits back again, she's closer, one little shift on the couch and her thigh presses against mine.

She bites her lip. Her eyes are focused on my mouth and a surge of heat rushes through me.

She inclines in my direction and I lean back. "Scarlett. Are you sure about this? You've been drinking."

A puff of laughter escapes her. "I've had a glass and a half over the past three hours, with food." She smiles and the small movement of her mouth is the end of any resistance I might have had. "And I know you said you could never be just friends with me and I think," she moves in closer, her eyes dipping to my mouth, "not-friends can make out sometimes."

And then she kisses me.

Chapter Thirteen

Seize the moment. Remember all those women on the 'Titanic' who waved off the dessert cart.
    —Erma Bombeck

Scarlett

I ALWAYS MAKE the first move, like an aggressive fiend, but something tells me Guy doesn't mind. Not when his lips are on mine, stroking in the softest way possible. This isn't like in the kitchen, or even the first time we kissed. It's not overwhelming and fiery, it's soft and sweet. Comforting. Like the spaghetti. His arms go around me and pull me closer and then somehow, we're lying on the couch stretched out and facing each other, my head on his shoulder and his resting on my bicep.

The heat doesn't escalate like I expected. His hands are around me, but he doesn't go for the goods like before, not like I might've expected. It stays like this, soft and sweet and no expectations.

He pulls back and I follow, seeking more.

"I never bring women here," he says.

"Never?"

"I have teenage girls. It's not exactly a den of iniquity. Not since . . ."

"Your ex-wife?"

He hesitates, searching my eyes for a few long seconds and then nods. "She wasn't the nicest person to them. Or me for that matter."

Surprise fills me. "Why wouldn't she be nice? I mean, I can see why you might deserve it," I tease. "But they are the sweetest girls."

He smiles, but it falls quickly. "Marie was raised a little differently. She was an only child and her parents are wealthy from some grandparent who struck it big in oil. She's never had to work or have goals or exist in a world where she wasn't the center of everything."

I try to picture Guy in a relationship with someone like that, knowing how hard he works, how hard he's worked to get to where he is, and I just can't see it. "I hope you don't find this question insulting but how could you have married someone like that?"

He shifts to rest his head closer. "I didn't know how she really was, initially. She was fun, beautiful, sweet and caring. I was riding the high from the reality show doing so well, and still kind of stuck in this . . ." he stops to think, trying to find the right words, "Hollywood version of reality. Reality shows aren't real, you know?"

I nod.

"It's all produced and dramatized to the point of fiction. Marie liked that version of me, the actor, the one that pulled in the ratings, and she was upset when I didn't want to go back. I'd spent too much time away from the girls, and now I sort of regret it. Except, I wouldn't be where I am now without having done it. But Marie, she acted unaffected by my choices and outwardly she was fine with the kids. I believed her when she said she didn't care I was raising the girls. It wasn't until Ava told me how she really was when I wasn't around that I had any inkling of anything being wrong. And then the full truth really hammered home when she tried to get me to send them away."

"Away where?"

"Boarding school for Ava and a special facility for Emma."

My whole face drops. "No."

His eyes shutter, gaze lowering. "It's my fault. I chose poorly, and I didn't prepare Marie adequately for the severity of Emma's condition because…I guess I never thought of it as a problem. She is who she is, and I love her for it."

I cup his face in my hands. "You're a good man."

His eyes search mine, the bright green dim in the low lights. "You might not think so tomorrow."

My mouth twitches. "Maybe not."

He leans in, pressing a gentle kiss to the corner of my mouth. One side, then the other. Then my cheek, the side of my jaw, and finally my nose. He pulls me closer and I snuggle into the crook of his neck. "Let's stay here forever," I say, breathing in the piney scent of him.

"Okay. We live here now." He glances around. "We might have to subsist on old Cheetos and cereal from underneath the couch cushions."

"I'm okay with that."

He grins wide and uninhibited, and it takes my breath away. Then he kisses me on the corner of my mouth, then my chin, his lips pressing more soft touches to my skin, until our mouths meet again, a gentle pressure that goes on until I don't know where I end and he begins.

WHEN YOU'RE A BUSINESS OWNER, there's no such thing as the weekend. Even on Sunday. I'm busy baking ahead to freeze, scheduling requests for catering into an already packed calendar, posting on social media with specials for the week…all while making sure I can pay my bills, and doing laundry in the creepy basement of my building. Laundry is the last thing I want to do, but I also don't want to stink if I happen to make out and fall asleep with Guy again. I shift in the rickety lawn chair that lives in the basement next to the washing machine and balance my laptop on my knees.

The thought of making out with Guy sends shivers up my spine and straight to my lady bits.

I can't believe we fell asleep on his couch together, wrapped up in each other, a cocoon of perfect bliss. We were awoken at 2 a.m. by Emma walking around the apartment, and then Guy ordered me an Uber.

I slept for a few hours and then woke up to get some work done. I should be exhausted, but I'm oddly energetic. Like the mere thought of Guy is a jolt to my system, an extra dose of caffeine straight to the veins.

Maybe I shouldn't be so lighthearted about this. Maybe I should be worried as I go through all my bills and expenses. After paying Fred's part-time wage, I'm barely squeaking by. I used trust money from my parents to purchase the truck, but that's nearly depleted since I've also had to use some of it for regular living expenses. It goes quick in New York City, even if you aren't living in a penthouse.

And asking my parents for more money? No way. They can't bother themselves to call me. They don't care at all about my life. They never have. I would rather move back to Blue Falls and deal with all the shame of failure than ever ask them for one red cent.

Maybe I need to think more about if Guy is going to really try and make me go elsewhere, just in case. Where else could we go? To be fair, he did say he would find something for me, but what if he can't? I mean, can this really end well?

He's the worst person for me to…have feelings for. Then again, every other man I've dated in my short life has seemed like the perfect match; look how well those relationships ended up. Maybe not-perfect is exactly what I need.

Despite all the potential landmines between us, I can't stop thinking about him and wondering what he's doing.

I respond to some messages on social media and then stare off into space at the concrete wall of the laundry room. Compared to Guy's apartment, this place is a real dump. These machines are from before I was born. Most of them only dry halfway even if you run them through two cycles, and the quarter slots don't always work properly.

Not that I can complain, having a roof over my head and being able to afford it in the city in a not-terrible neighborhood is an accomplishment in and of itself.

My phone dings with a text. I pick up my phone.

FRED: According to the doc I am now fit for public consumption. I can come in tomorrow.

ME: Are you ever fit for public consumption? That's questionable.

PHONE DINGS AGAIN, and I think it's Fred responding but when I pick up the phone, it's an unfamiliar number.

HEY. It's Guy. Carson told me to tell you that he didn't give me your number.

I LAUGH, suddenly breathless. My thumbs hover over the keyboard, heart pulsing a giddy tune in my chest.

ME: He's not doing that sort of thing a lot lately.

. . .

GUY: It would be annoying if it weren't so opportune.
   What are you doing today?

ME: Oh, you know, living the dream.

I TAKE a picture of my crossed legs propped up on the old washing machine and attach it to the message. Visible in the photo are my old ripped up jeans and converse, both of which are not a major contrast to the decrepit walls behind the beat-up washing machine that I think was manufactured in 1983.

ME: What about you? I type in and press send.

HE SENDS A PICTURE BACK. He's got a goopy green face mask on. Behind him, Emma and Ava have matching green faces and they're all making faces at the camera.

   I burst out laughing.

ME: Wow.

GUY: Yeah, I get pampered a lot since I live with two women.

                        .   .   .

I GRIN AT MY PHONE, and another message comes through.

GUY: You working at your truck tomorrow?

ME: Yes.

GUY: Maybe I'll see you.

I BITE MY LIP. *Not if I see you first!*

No, that's lame. I hit the backspace until the words are gone. *I hope you do.*

Ugh. I delete that one, too. I end up sending a smiley emoji. I'm so lame.

The next morning I'm a jumble of excitement and anticipation when I pick the truck up from the commissary and drive it over to the spot.

Guy's car isn't outside when I arrive, but it's early. I park the truck, turn on the generator and get to work. It's silly for me to be all, I don't know, expecting something romantic. Like him, waiting with a flower in his teeth. Naked. I shake my head. I've lost it.

I shove all naked Guy thoughts out of my head and make a valiant attempt to keep busy prepping cakes, doing inventory, and making coffee until the back-door swings opens a couple hours later.

It's Fred. "Hey, I need help with the very vegan vanilla

frost—" I cut off when she removes her sunglasses, pushing them to the top of her head.

"Fred?" She's stopped the doorway, wearing another fandom shirt I don't understand, this one has two guys in a car, and it reads, *Driver picks the music shotgun shuts his cake-hole.* Her eyes are red and swollen.

"Are you still sick?"

"No. I feel much better." Her voice is strange and stilted. "Thank you." And then she bursts into tears.

Chapter Fourteen

TIS AN ILL COOK THAT CANNOT LICK HIS OWN FINGERS.
   --William Shakespeare, Romeo and Juliet

Scarlett

I STARE at her in shock. Fred doesn't cry. She's all snark and strength. I'm the one who cries, and she consoles me.

It takes a few long seconds for me to realize this is actually happening and rush over to her, pulling her into my arms. She's holding a small white paper bag and I take it from her and put it on the counter.

"Are you okay? What happened? Are you hurt? Who died?" I keep hugging her and she, surprisingly, let's me.

"It's J-J-Jack," she manages before burying her head in my shoulder and breaking into more sobs.

"Jack died?!"

"No!" She pulls back, yanking a tissue from a pocket

and blotting her eyes. "He's not dead. Yet. He caught my bug and then he...he broke up with me." She sniffs. "It doesn't make any sense." She crosses her arms over her chest and stares at me with bewildered eyes.

"He broke up with you because he got sick? There had to be some other reason."

"It's...he...we . . ." She shrugs helplessly before tightening her arms around herself, as if the physical act can contain the emotions from further eruption. "Out of nowhere he was done, like he woke up one day with the sniffles and decided he didn't love me anymore."

"What did he say, exactly?"

Maybe this is delusion brought on by too much cold medicine.

"He said he didn't want to be with me anymore and I have to move out."

I blink at her. "Just like that?"

She shrugs. "Just like that. No real explanation. We talked in circles for what felt like hours. Me asking what happened and him sort of answering but not. Does that make sense?"

"Not really." I frown.

She lifts her hands in a futile gesture. "He kept saying he doesn't want to be an us anymore. Which means he doesn't want me."

Anger on her behalf makes my jaw clench. "He's the biggest fool in New York. You deserve better."

She steps away from me, gazing out the order window with a blank expression on her face. "It's just, it's always been the two of us. And he's always been weird, and I've been weird and I thought our weird matched, but I was wrong. Anyway, I have to move out. I never should have let him have control over all our things. But I thought, we were always a team, you know? And yeah, he's been working more but I never asked for anything more, I was happy to be with him. To take care of him. He said I could stay a couple weeks to give me time to find something, but I can't stay there, Scarlett. I have to get out as soon as possible."

"Do you need a place to stay? You can stay with me."

"No. I can't do that to you. I can go stay with my parents." She winces. "I might need to find a real job, though, so I don't have to live with them indefinitely."

"What would you do?"

She shrugs helplessly. "I don't know. But I'll figure it out. In the meantime, put me to work. I need to think about something else."

She walks over to the sink and washes her hands. We step around each other in the truck, the routine taking over our movements, but Fred doesn't stop talking.

"I can't afford to live in this city," she murmurs while loading trays of cupcakes into the Vulcan. She doesn't even do her normal, "Live long and prosper" schtick. "I hate it here," she continues. "I only stayed for Jack because I thought we would be together forever. I'm too strange. No one else will love me. What am I going to do?"

"Have you talked to your parents?"

"Yes. They still have a room for me. I only have clothes and incidentals at Jack's. Pretty much everything else in the apartment belongs to Jack."

"We can close up early. I'll go with you and help you

grab your things."

"I don't want you to lose business because of me."

I rub her upper arm. "It will be fine, Fred."

We open to get some of the after-lunch crowd, and while we're handing out cakes and taking money and making change, Fred is constantly wrapped up in her thoughts and they're coming out of her mouth.

"Why do we want love so bad, anyway? Is it really necessary? What is it about human beings in our biology that draws us to the promise of love and happy ever after? What if it doesn't exist? Love songs. Love books. It's always a subplot; I mean, look at Han Solo and Princess Leia, Cas and Dean shippers, et cetera. It never ends. Love is everywhere. We're obsessed."

I have no idea what shipping she's talking about, but okay. She's just rambling about her fandoms or whatever it is.

"We'll figure it out, I promise."

But her constant ramble is starting to prick at my own thoughts and insecurities about Guy.

Fred and Jack were together forever, and even though he wasn't perfect, I thought they loved each other. If even people who are together for a decade can end in heartbreak for no good reason, how could I possibly stand a chance? I'm overthinking things again. I mean nothing's even happening with me and Guy, we just kissed a little. We're not even a couple. It would be ridiculous to already be anticipating our breakup.

"What's this?" Fred asks when there's a lull in business. She's holding up the white bag I took from her when she first arrived.

"You had it when you came in. I thought it was yours."

She shakes her head and hands it to me. "It was outside on the bumper."

I take it from her and peer inside. There's a chocolate croissant wrapped in paper and a folded note. I peel it open.

CAN I take you to dinner later? I know a place that has fancy macaroni and cheese. Guy

I SMILE. His handwriting is perfect block script. That's just like him.

"Why are you smiling like a dope?"

I drop the smile. "It's a chocolate croissant. From Guy."

She grabs the bag from me and chucks it in the bin.

"What did you do that for?"

She rolls her eyes, a little spark of her former self returning. "Scarlett, don't be naïve, it probably has ex-lax or something in it."

I bite my lip.

Her mouth pops open before I can even get words together in my head to tell her anything. "What aren't you telling me? Have you been consorting with the enemy?"

"I don't want to ruin your perfectly good mope, but I think the pranks are done. After the whole salt-for-sugar issue."

I explain everything, how Guy helped with the

wedding catering, and then sent Carson to be my last-minute savior. Then I tell her about dinner, and how he was with his sisters. I don't tell her every little detail, as some of it is too personal and doesn't feel right to share. But I give her the gist. "He's like a whole different person than you would expect."

Fred is quiet when I finish and I sort of expect her to deride the whole situation, especially after all the "down with love" monologuing that's been happening for the past few hours, but instead she nods and says softly, "Maybe you should give it a chance. You and Guy."

"You really think so? Even though . . ."

"Just because I suck at picking men doesn't mean you should be lonely forever."

"You don't suck at picking men. You've only had the one. When you've made half a dozen bad decisions like I have, then we can talk. And besides, I'm not lonely."

"Oh, Scarlett, maybe you're not lonely, but you want love. You *love* love. Half your cupcakes are named things like Love Me Lavender and Romantic Raspberry. You're obsessed with weddings. You want to get married and have a thousand babies to spoil. You can be strong and independent and still want a partner and a family. Don't let your fear of getting hurt hold you back from your dreams, and from something that could be amazing. And Guy clearly isn't the total cretin we thought. Maybe he acts like a dick sometimes, but he probably needs someone just like you to make him less of a douche nougat. I can't think of anyone that could do a better job."

I don't know what to say after her speech. That's the longest, most sincere thing she's ever said to me. I move to stand next to her, leaning into her side. "Are you saying that maybe our weird matches?"

"Exactly." Her smile is small but it's there. I give her a hug and as we part, she glances out the window. "I think your weirdo is coming over to see you." She nods in the direction of Decadence and my gaze swivels outside.

Guy stalks across the lot and my eyes devour him. He's wearing dark jeans and a long-sleeved shirt. Such a simple outfit that would be so much better on my bedroom floor. Oh no, there's a pervert in my mind and he's rasping out terrible pick-up lines. I banish the internal creep and swing open the back-door right as Guy is lifting a hand to knock.

His eyes lighten when they meet mine, but he doesn't make any moves in my direction. Instead, he shoves his hands in his pockets. "Hi."

"Hi, yourself."

He breaks our stare and rocks back on his heels slightly. "Did you get my note?"

"I did. I actually saw it a minute ago."

"Oh. Are you free tonight?"

I glance behind me at Fred who's stabbing a cupcake with a spoon.

"Rain check? I promised to help Fred."

His eyes sharpen on me and his head tilts to find her in the truck behind me. "What's wrong with Fred? Is she still sick?"

"No, not that." I explain how she broke up with her long-time boyfriend and needs to move out quickly, hopefully before he gets home tonight so she doesn't have to see him, and how we're closing up early to get it done.

"We can do better than that. I can help."

"What do you mean?"

He shrugs. "I have people."

Fred appears next to me like a wired jack in the box. "Please, yes, help me. I need to get out of there, and I will take support from the devil himself if it means I can avoid Jack."

"Give me the addresses for pick-up and delivery. What size truck will you need?"

Fred blinks at him a few times and then answers his questions.

I glance back and forth between the two of them, Guy clipped and efficient and Fred, slow at first but then responding with increasing briskness to match his tone.

"I don't have much stuff, my clothes and toiletries and books. Some fandom merch. All the furniture and everything big belongs to Jack."

Guy nods. "I'll be back in thirty minutes."

And then he's gone, and Fred and I stare at each other with wide eyes.

"What just happened?" she asks.

I shrug. "Guy Chapman."

It's more like twenty-eight minutes before he's back. All I get is a quick smile and nod and then they're both gone. I could have done with a quick kiss. Even on the cheek. Maybe a hug? Maybe he's just not feeling it. I shove those thoughts to the side and continue to peddle my cupcakes and wait.

A couple of hours later, they return. Guy drops Fred off and then disappears. I squash a pang of disappointment that he didn't come in to say anything. Not even a smile and nod, this time.

"What happened?" I ask Fred.

"He said Jack is an idiot." Her eyes are brighter than they were this morning, her spark coming back in slow degrees. I owe Guy just for that. "It was epic, Scarlett. He took care of everything, I barely had to even think. I don't normally enjoy being bossed around, but he made something I was dreading just so easy."

I grin at her. "You've got it too, huh? The Guy Chapman Fan Club button."

She snorts. "You have a bigger button. Carson is right, he likes you."

I ignore that statement and the butterflies it creates in my stomach. "Do you need any time off?"

"No." She shakes her head and heads to the sink to wash her hands. "It's better if I stay busy. Work will help."

"Okay, well let me know if you change your mind."

She finishes washing up and dries her hands on a paper towel, turning to face me. "My parents invited you and Guy over for dinner and I agreed on your behalf, by the way. He's coming back in an hour to pick us both up."

"He is?" I squeak. I've been working and cooking all day. The truck gets warm, despite the chill outside. I put my hair up in a messy bun hours ago. My face is probably greasy and gross. I probably resemble stomped butt.

"Hope that's okay," Fred continues. "My parents are going to be so annoying and smothering. I need a buffer, just for a night. You don't mind, right?"

I shake my head no. I don't mind.

I guess I'm going to dinner with Guy tonight, after all.

Chapter Fifteen

ONE CANNOT THINK WELL, LOVE WELL, SLEEP WELL, IF ONE has not dined well.
   —Virginia Woolf

Guy

FRED'S PARENTS live in a brownstone in Park Slope. We're greeted in the entryway by Fred's mother, Helen, who takes our coats and hangs them on an antique wood coat rack in the corner.

"Scarlett, it's so nice to see you again." She kisses Scarlett on the cheek and then steps over to give me a quick hug.

I'm not quite prepared for the affectionate gesture. We just met for the first time earlier this afternoon. I'm lifting a hand to pat her on the back when she steps away and I almost snag a finger on the turquoise jewelry dangling from her ear.

"Larry, the kids are back," she calls out.

He yells something unintelligible.

"He's in the study reading the news and making himself upset." She rolls her eyes and steps back. "Come on in. Dinner is almost ready, and you will love it. It's my famous vegan chili."

Fred groans and walks past her into the kitchen. "Mom, it's only famous because of how much no one ever wants to eat it."

"It's very healthy and I put some quinoa in it this time so I think it will be better."

"Nothing can make it better."

Fred and her mother disappear into the kitchen, Scarlett and I trailing behind them. "I just love coming over here. They are as funny as all get out. I wish they were my parents."

I don't have a chance to talk to her more because Larry, Fred's dad, comes into the kitchen to greet us.

"Welcome back. I'm glad you guys could make it." He shakes my hand and hugs Scarlett before standing next to his daughter where she's leaning against the counter. "You got everything from that jackhole's apartment?"

"Yes, Dad." Fred sighs.

Her dad, I discovered earlier, works at Columbia University and he fits the image of exactly what I would expect of a tenured professor. Tall and lean, with salt-and-pepper hair, wire rimmed glasses that are fighting with bushy grey eyebrows, and a tweed jacket.

"Were you reading about politics again?" Helen asks him.

"Actually, I was reading about FRBs that are repeating in a consistent pattern."

"FRBs?" Scarlett asks.

Larry launches into a discussion about fast radio bursts, millisecond-long bursts of radio waves from space, and how normally when they repeat it's in a cluster or sporadic, but for over a year the same pattern has been recurring every 16.35 days.

"Sounds like aliens," Fred declares as soon as he's done explaining the finding.

"Don't make me hurt you." He points at her in a serious tone and Fred bursts out laughing.

"Come eat dinner, and no arguing about aliens over my famous chili." Helen ushers us into the dining room.

We sit around the comfortably appointed dining room, where the walls are a cheery yellow and the table is a chunky, dark wood. The discussion continues while Helen dumps chili into each of our bowls. Larry explains to the rest of us about neutron stars and what an OB-type star binary system is and how they are the likely culprit for the radio wave signals.

It doesn't stop Fred from teasing him about aliens while Helen laughs loudly.

"Did you want some cheese for your chili?" Helen asks me.

"Don't do it," Fred groans. "It's not real cheese."

"It's plant-based. I make it with oat and spices." Helen's smile is sunny and innocent.

"It tastes nothing like cheese," Fred grumbles.

"Well, it's not supposed to."

"Then why do you call it cheese?"

"Oh, you know, just for fun." Helen laughs again at Fred's disgusted expression. "Oh, stop being cranky. I know you're upset about Jack, but honey, you dodged a bullet."

"That boy was a self-absorbed jackhole," Larry mutters.

"I don't want to talk about it." Fred stirs her chili and staring down into it like it can erase the conversation.

"Fine," Larry says, then he turns to me. "So, Guy. What do you do?"

"Dad!" Fred gapes at him.

He lifts his bushy brows in confusion. "What?"

"This is Guy Chapman." Fred lifts an open palm in his direction, like she's Vanna White and I'm a row of lighted letters.

Larry stares at Fred for a second and then flicks his gaze to me, and then back at Fred, expression blank. "Am I supposed to know something here?"

I can't help but smile at all of them. In the restaurant business and maybe among reality show viewers, people know who I am. But to everyone else, I'm nobody, and I'm okay with that. I'm actually very relieved. "You aren't supposed to know anything," I tell Larry.

But Fred is undeterred. "He's a chef," she explains.

"Oh, okay. That's nice, son," Larry smiles at me encouragingly.

Scarlett strangles back laughter.

"Oh, that's just wonderful. Scarlett is a great chef, too." Helen clasps her hands in front of her. "I'm so glad true professionals can try my chili." She gives Fred a pointed look. "I'm sure it's going to be good this time."

It isn't, but I eat it anyway. "It's very…interesting. The flavors are unique."

I can't tell her the full, unadulterated truth. She's beaming at me and I can't hijack her happiness.

"See, I told you it was good. Scarlett, what do you think?"

Scarlett takes a delicate bite and nods solemnly. "I can honestly say I've never had anything quite like it."

Fred snorts. "Mom, they both agree it stinks, they're just saying it in a nice way."

"You've had a rough couple of days, so I won't give any credence to your words," she says primly.

After dinner, Helen insists we spend time with Fred while she handles the clean-up.

So, after arguing about clean-up for longer than necessary because of Scarlett's inherent sense of southern politeness, we go down to the basement. It's the only place in the whole brownstone with a TV, Fred tells us as we're stomping down the narrow stairs.

We descend into what could be a living room straight out of 1977. It's all fall tones, an old loveseat with orange flowers, wood paneled walls, a worn leather recliner and the most ancient TV I've ever seen.

"I wish your parents were my parents," Scarlett says to Fred.

"You can have them."

There's a bookshelf next to the TV, stocked with VHS tapes. Fred grabs one and puts it in. Then she throws herself into the recliner.

Scarlett and I sit on the loveseat. The space is small, and our thighs are only a few inches apart.

"What are we watching?" Scarlett asks as the opening credits come up on the screen.

"Teen Witch. It's a wonderfully terrible movie which perfectly fits my current mood."

Then Fred's mom calls her name, which she ignores until she's yelled three times and then finally Fred groans and pulls herself upstairs and we are left alone.

Scarlett adjusts slightly on the sofa, and our thighs touch. I tense, waiting for her to pull back, but she doesn't.

I glance around. "I didn't know places like this existed."

"Rooms that feel like you're back in time?"

I shake my head and give in to temptation to reach out and brush her hair back from her face where a deep red strand has fallen over her cheek. "Intact families that talk and eat dinner together every night and take care of each other."

"You have that."

My thumb traces a circle over the smooth skin on the side of her neck. "I don't have a partner, though. It's just me and the girls."

"I can relate. But there's still hope, it's just that some of us have to make our own families."

I search her dark eyes. "That's true."

Her head ducks briefly and then she looks at me from under her lashes. "Thank you for everything today. I'm glad you're here."

"So am I."

"Why *did* you help Fred?" Her face tilts to the side.

I hesitate, not anticipating the question and needing a moment to examine my motivations. "She was upset… and you were upset." It's the truth, but admitting it isn't easy. But still, I forge ahead even though a little voice inside is yelling *Stop now, danger ahead!* "And I guess…I just wanted to make you happy."

Her lips pop open in surprise.

I'm a little shocked, too. What am I doing? I don't bend over backward to help people in general, let alone those who are standing in the way of my goals. My life has always been about work—that's all that matters. It's what I can control. I don't bend to other people's needs—unless it's my sisters—and I definitely don't admit to weakness.

Oliver called me today, once again pushing for me to make some kind of move to get Scarlett out of the picture, and instead, I helped her employee move. What is wrong with me?

When did someone else's happiness begin to tangle with mine until I couldn't establish the difference?

She leans into me, closer.

My breath catches in my throat.

"Scarlett!" Fred's voice shrieky and closer than I anticipated.

We jerk away from each other, creating rapid distance like two recalcitrant teenagers caught by their parents.

"I brought down some wine." She plops down between us, setting the bottle on the coffee table. The seat is too small, and she doesn't quite fit, but she doesn't care.

"It's half empty," Scarlett points out.

"I had some. Mom made me." She hiccups. "She's a

bad influence in addition to being a terrible cook. What were you guys doing?"

"Nothing." We both answer too quickly.

She sighs and leans her head on the back of the couch. "I can't believe Guy Chapman ate my mom's chili. It's the worst thing anyone can think of. It's like showing my kindergarten finger painting to Picasso and expecting him to think it's fine art."

"It wasn't bad," I say.

"It was," Scarlett says.

We smile over Fred's head.

We stay and watch the movie for a little bit, and it's probably the most ridiculous thing I've ever seen while being simultaneously entertaining, but it doesn't take long before the wine catches up to Fred. The movie isn't even half over before she's leaned against Scarlett's shoulder, snoring like a champ.

We carefully extricate ourselves from around her, taking more care than necessary considering she keeps snoring throughout the whole ordeal.

Once we're free, I find a blanket in a chest in the corner and we settle it over her then shut off the TV and silently move up the stairs.

The upper floor is quiet and dark except for a small lamp in the entry, lighting our way. We grab our coats from the coatrack in the entry but before we can escape, Fred's mom appears from a side doorway.

"I put together some leftovers for you guys to take home with you." She hands us a couple of disposable containers.

"That's mighty kind, thank you." Scarlett smiles and takes them both.

Helen glances between the two of us. "Thank you both so much for spending time with Fred. She needs the distraction. Jack was her first everything and she hurts even more than she lets on. She didn't have a lot of friends growing up. Always had her head stuck in a book, living in a fantasy, and we might have encouraged her too much in that regard. Maybe we should have pushed her to be more social."

"Fred is a delight," Scarlett assures her.

Helen nods. "Yes, she is, but her outwardly gregarious personality is a bit of a show. She wants to make friends, but she's always struggled with finding her place and what she wants in life."

"I love Fred. I will always be here for her," Scarlett says.

"She loves you too, and it doesn't come to her easy. When she gives, she's all in. Unfortunately, she gave it all and Jack didn't know what a precious gift he had."

"Clearly," I mutter.

We finally say goodbye and exit the brownstone onto the dark and quiet street.

"I can take you home," I tell Scarlett as we walk down the sidewalk toward my car.

"Thank you."

The ride to her apartment in Washington Heights is silent, but comfortable. When I pull up outside her building, Scarlett turns to me.

"Did you want to come up?"

More than anything.

"I can't. I have to get home to the girls."

"Right. Sorry."

"No, don't be sorry."

She glances out the window and then back at me. "Thanks for the ride," she says. And before I can lean over the console or say anything else, she disappears out the door.

A FEW DAYS pass and I don't see Scarlett at all. We text, but that's it.

She's busy cooking for events, because even though it's almost Christmas, the holiday isn't slowing down her catering business. Decadence is as busy as ever and renovations are nearly completed for Savor, so we've started taking reservations there as well—even through the holiday season.

Ava asks me where Scarlett is and if she's coming over again, and I don't know what to tell her.

"I like her," Ava says.

"Me, too," is the only response I have.

Two days pass like this, two days that feel like thirty. But finally, on Wednesday, Carson comes in from lunch with a familiar pink container.

I stand in the doorway and watch him place the box at the corner of his desk.

"Is that from Scarlett's?"

"Yeah." He and shrugs out of his coat and hangs it on the back of his chair, unconcerned.

"She's there?"

He stops and lifts his brows at my tone. "Um. Yes."

I glance in the direction of the front door, like I can sense her through the kitchen and walls and everything else between us.

Then I turn back into my office and pick up my phone. We haven't talked since the night at Fred's, only texted updates about what we were up to at random intervals. Mostly impersonal, but friendly. Like we're friends. My jaw clenches. We can't be friends. We're rivals. Aren't we? I still need to figure out what to do with our competing interests. But my mind shies away from any of that to focus on…why hasn't she texted to tell me she's here?

"Is she busy?" I call out to Carson.

"Yes. They're always busy. Kind of like we are."

I put my phone down and try and shake off the weird sensations coursing through me. It's like an itch I can't reach.

If she can work and not worry about me, I can do the same.

But it doesn't last. A few more hours pass, dinner service is starting, everything flowing smoothly, and I'm ready to burst out of my skin. I call Clara and ask her to stay with the kids through dinner, just in case.

It's like she's become part of my habits and not seeing her makes me feel like I'm going to explode.

Carson leaves for the day and I can't take it anymore.

I grab my jacket and head outside. The back door of her truck swings open before I can make it all the way there. She saw me coming.

"Hi," she says. Her smile is shy and small, but all the

same, it relaxes something inside of me, a tense ball that's been coiling inside over the past two days.

"Hi." Now I can't stop smiling and she's beaming at me right back.

"Do you want some coffee or tea?" she asks. She's fidgeting and her nerves help calm me a little because it's not just me. I'm not alone in this.

I nod and follow her into the warmth of the truck.

She moves around the space easily, her hands going through the motions with ease, grabbing cups and pouring coffee.

I lean against the counter, watching her move. My body is swirling with a craving, an insatiable need that's been simmering for days, a pot ready to boil over. The need shakes me to the core. I want her with abandon, with every cell of my being. But it's too much. I want her to know exactly where I stand. I want her to know this is about more than attraction.

Slowly, she brings me a cup, stopping directly in front of me.

I take it from her and set in on the counter.

"Scarlett, we should talk—"

She shakes her head. "No."

And then she steps into me and lifts her mouth to mine.

Chapter Sixteen

GREAT FOOD IS LIKE GREAT SEX. THE MORE YOU HAVE, THE more you want.
    –Gael Greene

Scarlett

IT HAPPENED AGAIN. He was standing there, being all handsome and smoldery in his plain old jeans and t-shirt. Every little part of him flipped a switch inside me, a sexy switch. From the stubble covering the hard line of his jaw, to his serious expression and penetrating gaze lasered on me. I can't read him, but I want to, with my fingers. He's like a contained tornado or something—like the intensity pulses off him and reaches into my stomach, making everything clench and want. I missed him. I missed this feeling, the butterflies and the excitement of being around him. So, I take.

"I want you," I say against his mouth.

The past couple of weeks, heck maybe the past year, have been an exercise in sexual tension and I think I'm about to spontaneously combust from pure desire.

He releases a deep and heady moan and the flame between us turns into a bonfire lit with dry wood and extra gasoline.

His mouth is an intoxicating flame against mine, licking at my lips, moving down to my neck, searing across my jaw, driving me wild. Arousal thumps between my legs. Forget foreplay. There can be no opening act. I want the final show, and I want it now.

I jump up on the counter behind me and pull him closer. It's the perfect height for him to step between my legs and I wrap them around him, pulling his erection right where I need it most. But it's not enough.

I reach between us, fumbling at his zipper and he pulls back slightly to help me tug his pants down. He's wearing boxer briefs underneath and I yank at them, too, until I can grasp him with one hand.

"Scarlett," my name is a groan laced with a plea.

"I need fewer clothes." I wiggle on the counter, yanking my leggings down and off along with my panties. The steel counter is cold against my rear, but I barely notice it over the heat raging through my body.

I can't wait any longer, but there's one more thing. "Wait." I reach over, pulling a condom out of the drawer next to us.

He frowns at it and then meets my eyes. "You just have those…there?" He's breathing heavy, strangling back amused laughter.

"It's a long story. I don't, I mean, I haven't done this here at all. Or anywhere else lately, anyway, I mean, I guess what I'm saying is despite the fact that I have twenty condoms hidden strategically around this truck, I haven't actually been with anyone in a very, very long time." Saying it out loud is a little scary. Vulnerable.

"Hey." He takes my hands, kissing my fingertips and then running his palms up my arms. "Me either."

He leans in and his soft lips brush my neck.

"Really?" He's got to be lying, I mean, look at him. But I can't think with him nibbling at me like I'm edible.

He pulls back, his hands cupping my face. "Really. I haven't been with anyone in a while. Not since Marie."

My eyes meet his. I can't believe it. "No one?"

"No one."

"Not even, like, a one-night stand with a gymnast?"

"Nope. I have the girls, so I don't bring home strangers. It would confuse them. And oddly, I haven't met or had many women with condoms hiding in random locations when I needed it."

I shrug and lean my head back while he runs his nose up the side of neck, giving me shivers. "I like to be prepared."

"I really appreciate that." Soft kisses drop all over my skin like rain, peppering the corner of my jaw, underneath my ear, then his lips brush over my cheek, corner of mouth, sensitive hollow of my neck. "I really appreciate this, too," he murmurs. One hand slips up my inner leg and my breath falters.

"Guy." My voice catches when his fingers slip along the ridge of arousal, feeling how wet and ready I am for him. Sliding his knuckle up and down my folds, until I'm panting and moving my hips against him.

On a curse, he rips the condom wrapper with his teeth, and then he's there—hot and hard and I think I might kill him if he doesn't put it in me now, but he slows down, his head teasing my entrance.

"Guy," I repeat, his name on my lips is part whine and part demand. If he drags this out any longer, I might literally die. The craving sinks into my skin and takes up a pulse between my legs and everywhere.

Arms around him, I grip him around the waist hard. Hands clenching—and after a few torturous seconds of holding on and breathing, he moves. Oh so slowly, he presses into me.

My eyes fall shut.

He stops. "Scarlett." I force my eyes open and they lock with his, the bright green infiltrating my entire view.

Once our gaze is secure, he surges in the rest of the way and then stops, filling me up, his entire purpose directed at me, showering me like a wave.

"Heavens to Betsy," the exclamation comes out on a breath of air.

His head falls onto my shoulder and the warm puff of his laughter tickles the curve of my neck "Who is Betsy?" he lifts his head to meet my eyes.

"All the Southern I've tried to repress tends to fall out when I'm . . ." I search his eyes. "Overcome."

His smile is crooked and happy and something in my chest twists the longer we gaze at each other while he's seated inside me.

Then he starts thrusting, slowly pulling out and

driving back in, and I think I leave my body because nothing and no one has ever felt this good. I clutch his shoulders, running my hands down his back to his rear, yanking him closer. He smells like pine, mixed with the sugary vanilla scent of the truck.

He angles his hips and pushes into me, hitting the perfect spot, his lips trailing over my neck, lifting a thumb to my breast to gently tug at my nipple through my shirt, the motion pushing me right over the edge where I was hovering anyway.

I cry out, my arms going around his shoulders to hold him closer as the release pounds through me and then his pace increases and he shudders against me, tumbling over the edge.

I keep my eyes shut, my head in the crook of his neck, his arms around me while I wait for my breathing to moderate.

When my senses return, I lift my head and glance around. The back door is open a half inch. We still have on most of our clothes. This was a conflagration of passion. Everything I want and everything I fear. What if I could have it all? The passion and the love, the stable comfort…without losing myself in the process?

He pulls away and turns to dispose of the condom. I slide off the counter and blink dazedly, stuck in a post-orgasmic haze.

I'm never going to look at this counter the same ever again. I really need to remember to sanitize.

And with those thoughts come an avalanche of concerns. What have I done? I let myself get carried away, with dreams of hearts and sweetness and love, but I know better. This can't end well. He wants to get rid of me. What if he uses this as a piece of control? Just like every other person I've fallen for.

But then he's there, his arms coming around me and pulling me into his chest. "You need help cleaning up?"

I pull away slightly to scrutinize him. His green focus is warm, like a spring day in the middle of December.

"Yeah," I say.

He smiles at me and then grabs a napkin, kneeling on the ground in front of me. He cleans me up with soft but thorough swipes and then finds my panties and hands them over.

Being cared for with so much sweetness and attention does nothing but add another layer of terror. I can't lose this. It's almost worse than if he were perfunctory. This is something that will *hurt* once it's over. We haven't even discussed what we are! I should say something. We need to talk about this. Right? Isn't that what people do? Especially considering he still wants this property and I'm still parked on it. We just christened the site of our conflict for crying out loud.

I will not be a doormat people pleaser who avoids conflict. We will talk about this. I open my mouth to say something, but he beats me to it.

"Can I make you dinner?" His eyes flick between mine, a little crease between his brows while he watches me. "We can go down to Savor. No one is there."

He's nervous I'm going to say no. Am I not the only one putting myself on the line here?

We could talk about it over food, right? No harm in

that. I'm not running away again, I'm being proactive. And, besides, I am hungry.

I smile. "As long as it's not vegan chili, I'm in."

———————

WE BARELY MAKE it into Savor before I jump him again. This time, we do it right inside the kitchen door, up against the wall, I stashed some condoms in my bra before we locked up the truck.

It's his fault, really. He wouldn't stop touching me. He held my hand, rubbing his finger across the back of my thumb, kissed my knuckles, pulled me into his side, rubbed a piece of hair between his fingers—all of that just on the short walk between my truck and his building.

"What are you doing to me?" he murmurs in my ear after we finish and I'm limp against his chest.

"Whatever it is, you're doing it right back."

I follow him into the kitchen. He hands me his chef jacket. It's clean and undamaged. I pull it around my shoulders. "You got the burn marks out?"

"It's a new one. Sit here." He pulls out a stool and I sit a few feet away from the stove while he moves around the space, grabbing a knife from the wall, and finding a chopping board. He disappears into a walk-in fridge and then returns with a tray full of stuff.

I could watch him forever. Even his chopping is sexy, his hands moving with fluid grace, forearms flexing while he slices veggies with ease. Crushing garlic with the flat of his blade and tossing it in the pan. Aromas fill the space and my stomach rumbles.

"What are you making?"

"Chicken and seasonal veggies in a lemon garlic sauce."

He tosses the food in the pan like the pro he is, and I appreciate the muscles of his forearms and wonder how long I have to wait until I can jump him again.

"Here." He turns to me, holding up his spoon for me to taste.

I watch him while wrapping my mouth carefully around the utensil and then flick my tongue out to make sure none of the sauce lingers on my lips. His eyes trace the movements, the green darkening to viridian.

With a quick intake of breath, he turns back to the stove and finishes the meal, plating it with practiced hands and then pulling up a stool next to mine.

"Bon appetit."

"This smells amazing."

We eat and talk—about the girls, about the holidays —all while carefully avoiding any topic of conflict, even though I should bring it up. But every time I get up the nerve, my tongue sticks to the roof of my mouth.

It doesn't help that he's constantly touching me. Squeezing my knee, running a hand up my arm, cupping the side of my face in his palm and leaning in to kiss the corner of my jaw, even as I'm chewing.

"You're going to kill me," I tell him when heat floods into my nether regions, yet again.

"Really?" He takes my hand and puts it over his burgeoning erection.

My grin is uncontainable. "Again?"

"I find myself in this state basically whenever you're around. I don't know if I could ever get enough."

My heart melts in my chest and some emotions lumps in my throat.

"I almost forgot something to drink. Do you want some wine? I have some nice vintages—we need something good because this feels momentous. Doesn't it?" His brows dip and he stops to watch my reaction to his words. "Tell me if it's just me."

I blink at him in surprise. "It's not just you," I admit, heart pounding. Waiting for him to laugh and say he was kidding or something.

But he doesn't.

He smiles. It's large and the rare dimple makes an appearance.

Heat rushes straight south. I want to do him again. Now. Here. Wherever, really.

I shake my head. "You have to stop smiling at me or we'll never leave this room, and I didn't bring another condom."

He disappears for a second around the counter, voice muffled while he rummages in the wine fridge. "Why didn't you?" he calls out.

"Bringing one was wishful thinking."

"You could go get a couple more and grab some dessert while you're at it."

"Any flavor preference?"

"I would really like to try the 'Guy Chapman is a Butt-Sniffing Douche Double Chocolate with Nougat'. I've heard good things."

I laugh. "It's a best seller."

We smile at each other like a couple of dopes.

"Hurry back," he says.

"Right. Be right back." Flustered, I turn to the door and push my way through. I'm excited. Drinking wine and eating cupcakes and having more sex sounds like the best version of heaven I could imagine.

I hug his thick chef coat around me. It smells like him, the extra fancy forest, and I'm inhaling it, stepping out into the cold.

"Is Guy here?"

My smell party is halted by a feminine voice.

A throaty, sexy voice. She's tall, with cheekbones that could cut glass. Dark, perfectly highlighted hair waves around her face like she's just come from a salon. I don't know anything about fashion but whatever she's wearing is like something you can't even buy in stores yet because she yanked it off the runway. The woman is gorgeous. My hair is all day work followed by sex hair. Which, although it might sound hot and torrid, is really a jumbled frizzy mess. And I didn't even put on mascara this morning when I woke up at three am.

My thoughts are swirling and I only half register the taxi pulling away from the curb.

She's waving a hand in front of my face. "Hello? Is Guy Chapman in there?"

"He's…inside." The words are forced through suddenly cold lips.

She sizes me up, her eyes lingering on Guy's jacket hanging loosely from my shoulders. She smiles dismissively, maybe even a little condescendingly. "Thanks." She moves past me, but then stops and turns before she makes it more than a few steps. "You might be wearing his jacket but I'm still his wife."

I stand there like a statue and watch as she disappears into Savor.

The words don't register at first, like a dog barking nonsense in my mind, but then they do and I'm a little shocked. Still his wife? *Still?*

Was she lying? What if she wasn't? I glance back at the door quizzically.

How did she know he was here? This restaurant isn't even opened yet.

I should go in there and ask. But I don't think I can face him, not standing next to the glamazon supremo. He would look between the two of us and realize what a huge mistake he's made.

Do I even have a right to demand an explanation? We aren't even…I mean we just slept together, and it was intense, and he said it was momentous, but he's never promised me anything. He's never even said he wants to be exclusive, and here I am jumping in bed with him. Not even bed, a counter. I jumped on the counter with him. And the wall. And ugh I keep making the same mistakes over and over.

But is it a mistake? It's not one-sided. I didn't imagine the sweetness, the private side he only shows to me and to his sisters. I should trust my gut.

But past history considered, my gut is usually an idiot.

Okay, I've got it. I take a few deep breaths.

I'm not going to jump to conclusions. I hate it when people do that. I'm just going to go in there and ask him what's up like a normal adult would.

I stalk back to the door and then stop with my hand on the handle. But...what if they're making up? What if I walk in on...in my imagination, he's taking her up against the wall instead of me.

I shake the image off. It's not happening.

One more decp, calming breath that does nothing at all to calm me, and I shove back into the warmth of the restaurant.

Chapter Seventeen

CHEFS LOVE TO HAVE THAT CONTROL AND POWER TO CONTROL the message they want to deliver.

    –Steve Chen

Guy

I'VE HAVEN'T EVEN PULLED the glasses down when the door sweeps open. "That was fast. I hope you brought me one of the douche nougat—" I turn around, expecting to see Scarlett, but it's not.

It's, "Marie?" Standing in my kitchen like she thinks she belongs there. She takes off her coat and lays it on the counter.

"Who were you expecting, that woman in your chef jacket? You've taken to bringing conquests here, huh? Too crowded at home, I expect. So. Who is she?"

I don't bother answering her questions. It's none of

her business, although it rankles to hear her call Scarlett *that woman*, when she's so much more. And conquests? She has no idea. "What are you doing here, Marie?"

"I'm not allowed to stop in and see my husband?"

"You and I both know it's in name only."

As soon as the words leave my lips, something just outside pings and then crashes against the floor.

Marie smirks and opens the door to reveal Scarlett, who is holding my chef's jacket in one arm and clutching at a painting, which appears to have fallen off the wall.

"Scarlett?" Her face is red, and she won't meet my eyes.

Panic thumps through me.

I'm sure she heard most of our conversation and I want to punch myself in the face. I should have told her the truth sooner. Of course, Marie ran into her on the way in and did her best to set up the dice to fall for this exact outcome.

Scarlett is attempting to put the picture back on the wall. "Sorry, I was just…ah, bringing back your jacket and I need my keys. But then I ran into the wall but . . ." She struggles to lift the piece back onto the hanger, but she can't reach the hook.

I move toward her, "You don't have to—" but before I can reach her, she leans it carefully against the wall on the floor.

"Never mind. I'll get out of your hair. You guys probably have a lot to talk about." She steps back and turns but nearly runs into the wall again.

"No…wait." I glare at Marie. "Stay here, please." I go out the door, shutting it behind me, taking Scarlett's elbow and leading her away a bit in case Marie is listening. Of course, she's listening.

Scarlett steps out of my grip and gazes up at me, big dark blue eyes haunted. The pain in her eyes is a straight stab to the gut. "You're still married."

I rub the back of my neck. "Technically, yes."

Her arms cross over her chest and her eyes skitter to the side.

"But only because the State of New York won't accept divorce papers by reason of abandonment until a year has passed," I add quickly. "And it'll be a year within a matter of days. We've just been waiting to file. Which is probably exactly why Marie is here now."

She still won't meet my eyes. "I see." She's calm. Too calm. Like the eye of a storm.

"No, you don't. It's a long story. I'm sorry. I should have told you—"

"No." She cuts me off with a swipe of her hand and then takes a deep breath. "It's okay. I'm not mad. We can talk later. You have more important things to deal with. Just . . ." She bites her lip and still, still won't meet my eyes. I want nothing more than to take her in my arms and tell Marie to go to hell, but she's not wrong. It can't be a coincidence that Marie would show up now, when I'm so close to being able to file papers against her.

"Call me later." She finally meets my eyes, her expression remaining guarded.

"I'll come over," I say impulsively.

Her responding smile is small, but it's there and the sight of it gives me hope I haven't totally wrecked the tenuous connection between us. "What about your sisters?"

Dammit, she's right. I promised Ava I would be there before they went to bed.

My hands clench at my sides, wanting to reach out and grab her or kiss her, but I don't want to push it. She's pale and the smile is gone. I don't blame her. She found out I'm still married, and I know this must be hell for her, especially after her last boyfriend was married. And yet, she's not being dramatic or angry, she's being more understanding than I would expect from anyone.

"I'll be going, then . . . bye." She hands me my coat and then turns away.

I run a hand through my hair and watch her disappear out the front door.

I stand in the dark and empty restaurant for a few seconds, gathering my thoughts and emotions. I need to be clear headed to deal with Marie and her particular brand of behavior. She likes to make up her own narrative, the one that paints her as the biggest victim and everyone else is wrong and she's always right, and with that kind of thing? You've got to be on your toes, or she'll talk you right into a corner.

I'm worse than a douche nougat, even worse than ever before and I deserve something terrible to happen to me, but something terrible is happening and she's standing in my kitchen.

I've got to make this quick, keep her to the point. With all that in mind, I stride back into the kitchen.

"Did you come by to sign the divorce papers? I have them in my office."

She grimaces. "Do we have to talk about all that depressing stuff? I haven't seen you in a year." She reaches out to put a hand on my arm, but I step back. Her smile falters, but only for a flickering second and then she dials the charm back on. "Tell me how you've been."

"I'm not really in the mood to socialize."

"Aren't you? Isn't that what you were doing?" She waves at the plates, still sitting on the counter and she bites her lip and it reminds me of Scarlett, biting her lip because I hurt her. Marie's move is infinitely more orchestrated, something she rehearsed in the mirror to make sure she could pull it off to maximum effect. "I'm sorry I interrupted your evening."

"Are you?"

She sighs. "Come on, Guy. I'm not unreasonable. I'll sign the papers."

It's got to be a trick. "Really?"

"I thought we should have one more hurrah before it's over. You know, celebrate the way we used to."

"Sorry, Marie. It's over."

"Well." She offers me a mischievous smile and runs her eyes up and down my form. "Maybe if you don't fuck me again, I won't sign those papers. That might put a little damper on your…whatever you have going with the frumpy nobody. What do you see in her, anyway? I mean, if you're gonna move on from me it should be with someone important."

Scarlett is important.

She's everything.

And I might have totally fucked it all up.

"No."

She steps closer. "I'm sure we can compromise. C'mon Guy. This is how marriage works."

"You're insane."

"You love my insanity."

"I'm not sure I ever really did."

Hurt flashes in her eyes. Her head turns away and her hair falls over the side of her face, blocking her from my view.

"No one ever does." She releases a small laugh. "I thought we really had something, Guy." She smiles at me wistfully and for a second, I remember how it was, before. The woman I fell for, the one who could let down her guard and be her true self instead of the one she thought the world wanted. I knew she had some baggage when we met. Sheltered, abandoned by her parents and raised mostly by nannies and house staff, there's a reason she is the way she is. The problem is, she can't change.

"We did. And I'm sorry, Marie, but it's over." I make an attempt to gentle my tone, but it doesn't matter. It's a rejection either way.

Her head snaps up. Her voice is sharp when she responds. "Fine. Be a prude. All I want is this one little thing. But if you would rather not, it's fine, I'll just drag everything out in court. You know, the longer we're married, the more alimony you have to pay in the state of New York."

Anger vibrates into my bones. How dare she? She knows every penny I don't spend on essentials goes to a trust for the girls. But I doubt she really thinks about it. She doesn't need my money, never has.

I stare at her, unblinking, guarding my roiling

emotions like a wall. "If you don't sign, I'll get Oliver involved." I don't want to owe the bastard any more favors, but even that price is worth getting rid of Marie once and for all.

Marie's bravado immediately falters and her face pales. "You wouldn't."

Damn. What does Oliver have on her? "You want to bet on it?"

She stares at me, all of her earlier bluster and swagger gone. Poof. "Fine," she barks, picking up her coat where she left it on the counter. "Have your attorney send something over."

She shoves through the door and is gone, like an earthquake that lasts less than a minute but leaves a year's-worth of destruction in its wake.

I slump back against the counter and press the bottoms of my palms to my eyes, trying to quell the headache forming there. How did I ever fall for her act? She wasn't like this. She was sweet and funny before everything turned. But now I can see through the bullshit, more clearly than before. What she strives for isn't really important. Life isn't about being seen in the gossip rags, or reality shows, or followers on social media. Yes, in my business optics are important to an extent, but I want people focusing on the food and not me. I'm not that person anymore. I want to spend time with my family and people I care about. And Scarlett is now a part of that.

A sharp ache twists in my chest.

Hopefully.

By the time I get home to see the girls, it's their bedtime. We say goodnight to Clara and I ready them for bed. Then I go to the living room and try to breathe through the heaviness in my chest that's as big as a boulder. I can't stop seeing Scarlett's haunted expression before she left. Like her heart was breaking, but it was no more than she expected.

I am not like one of her exes and I don't want this, whatever it is between us, to be over.

My thumbs hover over the keys to tap out a text.

I'M SORRY.

I BACKSPACE, deleting the words.

I DIDN'T MEAN

I DELETE THOSE, too. A text will not suffice for this conversation.

Before I can second guess myself, I push the call button and press the phone to my ear.

It rings. Once. Twice. Three times. Fuck. And then—

"Hello?" her voice is low, the word a little fuzzy around the edges.

"Did I wake you?"

She sighs. "No. I was just lying here."

"I'm sorry. About Marie and everything."

I count her soft breaths. One. Two. Three.

"I'm not sure if you have anything to apologize for," she says softly.

"I do. I haven't even seen Marie in nearly a year, but we are technically still married. She's been putting off signing the papers because that's just like her. I think she will, now. It's only paper at this point. This thing between us, you and me, it happened so quickly…. But still. These are just excuses. I should have told you."

She's quiet for a few long seconds and my heart almost stops before she speaks. "Should you have, though? We aren't in any kind of serious thing."

Her words are true, I suppose, but it doesn't stop a lance of panic from shooting straight through my heart. To refer to what's between us with such indifference . . . the sense of wrongness grows, filling my chest and making my head pound.

"Aren't we?" I ask.

"We haven't," the words catch in her throat, "we haven't really talked about what we are."

"That's true. Maybe we should talk about it." I know she's attracted to me, but she's like a spooked horse. And this whole thing with the restaurant and her food truck…. It's an unresolved issue I'm determined to resolve to both of our benefits. I just don't know how. And in the meantime, I want her more than I want anything else. I'm half-tempted to give her the parking space, my restaurants, my staff, and my heart. But it's too soon and too scary to say those words out loud.

"Friends?" she asks.

I grimace. "Maybe something slightly more than that?"

"Friends who have the best sex in the known universe?"

I chuckle and the weight in my chest lightens a notch. "In the known universe, huh? That's a hefty title to live up to."

"Something tells me you're up to the challenge."

I hesitate. "And friends who only have this amazing sex with each other and no one else?"

She gives a quiet chuckle, and the weight pressing on me is nearly gone. "I think I can handle that."

"Well, that's something."

We sit on the phone in silence for a few long seconds, just listening to each other breathe. I don't want to sever the connection. I wish she was here. But I also don't want to push it.

I clear my throat. "I'll see you tomorrow?"

"Yes."

We hang up and I'm lighter and heavier at the same time because a realization occurs to me, latching its tentacles around the weird feeling in my chest and sinking into it like fingers sinking into putty.

I've only known Scarlett for a few weeks...not counting the first time we actually met a year ago. But it would pulverize me if she left—even more so than when Marie left. That was a dark time, but it's a speck of dust compared to my feelings for Scarlett.

With Marie, it was all passion and excitement, but it was surface. We never talked about anything serious. She never talked to the girls, never really made an effort. With Scarlett, the passion is there, but it's more. She's like a sun shining through all the dark spots in my life. She's present. She makes an effort for everyone around her, like she really cares. And I want to be around her, not just because of the sex but to see what she'll say. She makes me laugh. She makes me feel. It's invigorating and terrifying in equal measure.

THE MORNING IS HECTIC. Permits are coming through for Savor, which means we can open as soon as next week. I tell Oliver the good news and then press him for details on what kind of information he has on Marie that makes her run scared, but he's not talking.

Then Oliver presses me about getting the lot purchased—again—and I have to think quick to put him off.

I want to have my cake and eat it too, literally, but I don't know how. I tell Oliver I'm working on it and it will all be taken care of when Savor opens. That's a lie that I hope to become a truth. Somehow.

When we hang up, stress is thumping a dull ache in my temples, but I shake it off. I want to see Scarlett, but it's not until after lunch I can catch a break.

"Go see her."

I glance up to see Carson standing in the doorway.

"She's open. And you've been a cranky ass all day."

"Fine."

He doesn't have to tell me twice.

In less than a minute, I'm out the door and striding to her truck.

Fred is at the window, taking orders, and she yells into the back as I approach.

"Romeo, twelve o'clock," Fred calls out.

"Thanks, Fred."

The sound of her laughter-infused voice has me wound tighter than a spring.

The backdoor swings open and then Scarlett is there and she's in front of me, smiling wide. "Hi."

"Hi."

Seeing her makes everything in my body uncoil, and a new tension fills the space. "Do you have any plans for dinner tonight?"

She fidgets with her apron. "Actually, I have plans with Fred and Bethany."

"Oh." Is she putting me off because of everything that happened last night?

But then she's quick to reassure me, reaching out a hand and placing it gently on my arm. "It's not what you think; I do want to have dinner with you. I just can't tonight. Maybe tomorrow?"

"I can't." I rub the back of my head. "Ava has a school concert."

"Well, maybe Fred can switch our plans?" She turns, her voice hopeful. "We can go out tomorrow night instead of tonight."

"No can do. There's a new episode of Doctor Who on tomorrow night."

"You can't adjust our plans because you want to watch some show?"

Fred spins around, mouth agape. "Some show? How dare you?"

I interject. "It's okay. Night after tomorrow."

Her smile washes away the stress of the day. "Then it's a date."

"I'll pick you up at seven thirty."

"Okay." She's still smiling.

"Dress warm."

"Okay." The smile grows.

We stare at each other, my cheeks are hurting, and I wonder if my smile appears as goofy as hers and decide it most likely does, especially as I'm leaning toward her and Fred groans in the background. "Barf. Would you two get a room?"

I'm still going in for a kiss, but Fred's words jar Scarlett enough that she leans to the side like she's going in for a hug and we end up performing some kind of awkward half embrace and bungle the whole thing.

Scarlett bursts out laughing, and I pull away before I can make this situation even worse.

"I'll see you."

"Bye," Scarlett says.

Fred calls out "Bye Guy!" Then in a lower tone that I can still hear, she says to Scarlett, "Your weird totally matches."

I'm too giddy, already thinking about where to take Scarlett to wonder what she means.

Chapter Eighteen

AFTER A GOOD DINNER ONE CAN FORGIVE ANYBODY, EVEN one's own relations.

—Oscar Wilde

Scarlett

I'M a nervous Nellie by the time Guy calls up to my apartment right at 7:30. Jittery like a June bug.

"Be right down," I say into the speaker.

I take one last glance in the mirror. I didn't want to dress too fancy, but not too slovenly, either. Plus, it's frigid outside, so after trying on forty-five different outfits, I settled on a nice green sweater—for the holidays—with dark wash jeans and close-toed heels.

Grabbing my hat and scarf on the way out, I lock my door and head down the stairs. Guy wanted to come up, but I didn't really want him to see my apartment. It's small and a total mess of dishes and baking supplies. I've been trying out new flavors and frostings and I had no time to clean it up.

When I open the front door, he's there, waiting curb-side next to a sleek black town car. He's wearing dark pants with a blue button-up shirt and leather jacket. It fits him to perfection, hugging his form like it was made for him—and it likely was. I've seen him in a tux, in sweat shorts at home, jeans and Henleys, but this…this is different from his day to day hotness. It's like mega hotness to the nth degree.

He opens the back door and I pause for a quick embrace, leaning into him for a second, breathing in his piney scent before slipping past him into the car.

He slides in after me and tells the driver we're ready.

"I brought you something." He reaches down and grabs a small box and hands it to me.

I open it to reveal a chocolate covered cannoli and I gasp in pleasure. "It's like you can read my mind. I much prefer sweets to something like flowers."

I hand it back to him. "We might have to save it for after dinner, though. And I'll only eat it if you'll share it with me."

"Nervous?"

"A little." The lights from outside illuminate his face but the shadows make his eyes unreadable. "Also, I don't want to snarf food all over myself in front of you. I get crazy around desserts."

"I've noticed. I had eggs spread on my face once."

I laugh and smack him lightly on the shoulder. "Hey, it wasn't my fault. You instigated that one."

The curve of his cheek is like a reward. "I may have."

I glance out the window. "Where are we going?"

He hesitates. "It's a surprise."

"Can I guess?"

"If you must."

I bounce in my seat with excitement. "You're taking me to the top of the Empire State Building."

"Like in that movie? You think that's romantic? It's freezing up there right now."

I laugh. "Brent took Bethany there on their first date. Not to the normal observatory, but to the 102nd floor, before they even opened it to the public."

"That's a pretty good date idea. But it's not where I'm taking you."

I tap my lip. "Are you taking me to...a dumpster in Queens where Joe the hobo lives and serves fried rats with a side of wet garbage?"

He lifts both hands. "You caught me."

"I knew it!"

He laughs. "Your two guesses are the Empire State Building and a dumpster. Don't you think there might be something in between?"

I wrinkle my nose. "Those guesses aren't as fun."

He grimaces. "That's not boding well for me."

I lean closer, his heat a comforting pressure along my side. "I wouldn't care if you were taking me to a dumpster. I'm just happy to be here. With you."

He stares down at me. His mouth moves but nothing emerges.

And then the car pulls to a stop. He slides out turning to hold a hand out for me.

I slide out behind him, hoping I didn't ruin everything by being too honest. It's probably so obvious I haven't dated in forever.

"Oh." I laugh and clap my hands over my mouth. "Did you seriously bring me to eat at a food truck?"

We're outside the entrance to LuminoCity—a theme park full of colorful Christmas inflatables and lights. Parked to the side are a row of food trucks.

He shoves his hands in his pockets and his smile is small and sheepish, but it's there. "They have excellent food. Come on. We can see the lights afterward. I brought the girls here last week and they loved it."

I shake my head but follow him over to a Salvadoran truck. We get in line behind a family of four; a little girl in pigtails yanks on her dad's hand and loudly asks for donuts.

"How was Ava's concert last night?" I ask him.

"It was good. An hour of middle schoolers playing Hot Cross Buns, the Appalachian Hymn, and Home on the Range."

"Exciting."

He shrugs. "It wasn't bad. Emma enjoyed it. And I'm happy I can attend their events. I missed a lot when I was doing the reality show. I missed too much, and I regret it."

I don't have a chance to respond to that statement because it's our turn. We put in our orders and then step over to the pick-up window.

"You're doing what you can, now, though. That's something you should be proud of," I tell him.

He rocks back on his heels and rubs the back of his neck. "Thanks."

We take our food over to a little table and dig in. The pupusas are delicious, stuffed with cheese and covered in pickled jalapeños and coleslaw.

"What are you and the girls doing for Christmas?" I ask him.

He's methodically cutting up his pupusas into bite-size sections. "Breakfast at Rockefeller Center with Santa. It's a tradition. They love it. You?" He spears a piece of pupusa with his fork and eats it, his eyes on me.

"Heading home to Blue Falls."

"With your parents?

I chew my food before responding. "No. Just Granny and Reese. I don't know where my parents will be. I think their art show is tonight, actually, in Harlem."

"You mentioned that. They never extended an invitation or called you or anything?"

"Nope."

His green eyes watch me, searching. "Are they really that bad?"

I consider the question for a second. "It's hard to describe, it's probably more of my problem than theirs, really. I wish they cared a little more, you know? They aren't bad people. They've never lifted a finger to me. Never yelled or anything. I almost wish they would, because it would mean they cared."

I don't think I'm explaining it right. Guy's brows are drawn down.

I try again, fidgeting with a napkin on the table. "They aren't evil. It's just that they don't care about things other than themselves. I want them to like me, you know? To reach out or try and feign some kind of interest. Like I actually matter."

"Have you ever talked to them about it?"

I shake my head. "No. I don't think they would listen, or care."

He picks up my free hand and laces our fingers together and my heart flips a couple times. "Maybe the conversation isn't entirely for them. Maybe it would help you, just to get it out there and off your chest."

I stare down at our linked fingers. "I called my mother's cell, just to say hi, but got her assistant. They always have some up-and-coming aspiring artists help them out, and they're never very good assistants because they are as self-absorbed and scattered as my parents. Anyway, I told him—Alonso or something—that I was in town if they wanted to meet up, and he said, 'Okay Sansa,' and hung up on me."

He lets out a short, surprised laugh. "Sansa? That's not even close to your name."

"That's what I said, but Fred said maybe he really likes *Game of Thrones*? I guess it's a character from the show."

His hand squeezes mine gently. "Don't limit yourself because of what other people think. Not even your parents. They don't know you and it's their loss because you are an amazing human and stronger than you know. You are enough."

And when he says it like that, without wavering, I almost believe it.

I change the subject back to Granny and Reese and the upcoming holidays.

We finish eating, throw away our trash and then head into the park.

"That food was amazing." I groan, rubbing my stomach.

"I know." He holds out his arm and I take it, relishing the feel of his fingers closing over mine, pulling me firmly to his side.

I smirk at him. "I knew it. You do like food trucks."

He turns his head speaking low and close, like he's telling me a secret. "I have a thing for their owners, too."

His breath tickles my ear and my stomach does a thousand flip flops in three seconds, flat. "Do you now?"

He stops suddenly and then without warning turns me into him and brushes his lips over mine, shooting a thrill straight down my stomach and all the way to my toes. I blink up at him, wanting more than anything to continue in this direction—the one where our lips are touching and maybe our arms, chests, legs and hey maybe we could take off our clothes, too—but then a group of people jostle around us and we break apart.

Breathless and dazed, I can do nothing but follow as he tugs me along the walkway.

We spend a couple hours traipsing around the amusement park.

There is an enormous white and blue castle, flashing with lights. We walk, pressed together, through the Frosted Forest, an icy valley full of penguins and polar bears, and through a colorful mushroom forest.

The whole time, I'm trying to focus on the displays, but Guy is touching me. My arm in his elbow, his other hand playing with my fingertips. Or, his hand on my back.

Once, he tugs me behind an LED-lit tree to kiss the side of my neck. He's waging a war, but there are no casualties, only an onslaught of tender moments.

I'm about ready to traumatize some small children if he doesn't stop or get us out of here.

"Do you want to see the Sweet Dream and Candy Station?" he asks, pointing down the last section of lights.

"I would rather be alone."

He frowns and I realize how the words sounded.

"I mean, not alone, by myself. Alone with you." I wince. "I'm ruining the moment, aren't I?"

He chuckles and pulls me closer, his eyes dropping to my mouth.

"We could be alone," I say, the words coming out in a rush. "I have an empty apartment. Just don't judge my dirty dishes. I've been experimenting with flavors."

His eyes search mine intently and then the corner of his mouth tips up. "I'll call the car. Then I'll have to call Clara." He gives me a gentle tug and I follow him back down the path, toward the exit.

"Oh, will you have to go home soon?" I ask.

I get it, but…I'm simultaneously disappointed and understanding, an odd mix when it's also combined with the insatiable need to get him undressed as soon as possible and touch his naked body as much as I can for the foreseeable future.

He stops and faces me, the white glow of nearby lights flickering over his features, outlining his jaw, shadowed in stubble. "I hope it's not too presumptuous, but I already asked her to stay overnight with the girls. I just have to call and let her know."

I'm already shaking my head. "Not presumptuous. Smart. Wonderful. Welcome." I lean into him, pressing kisses to his lips, then cheek, then the prickliness of his jaw.

He tilts his face down to mine so our foreheads are touching. "I have to leave by eight tomorrow morning."

"That's fine, I have to get up early anyway." I lean in again, wanting more right now and he stops me.

His hands cup my face. "I want to make sure you understand this is not just about getting my rocks off and sneaking out in the morning. I've never been the kind of person who can do that, or thought the act was insignificant. I know we sort of already agreed to be exclusive, and I meant it."

"So," I bite my lip, "You're saying you're a serial monogamist?"

He nods. "If I'm with you, it's only you."

I'm stunned for a minute because with all my bad dates and past boyfriends, none of them ever talked like this. This is what I've always wanted. I never thought I would find someone who felt like me. But here he is.

I slide a hand up his chest to his jaw. "How fast can your driver get us back to my place?"

I swallow and his eyes track the movement. His brows lift and a grin tugs at his mouth. "Really? All this talk of monogamy is turning you on?"

"You have no idea."

He leans in to whisper in my ear, "Exclusivity, commitment, stability . . ."

My hand clenches on his arm. "Stop or I won't be able to wait."

The sound of his laughter is both satisfying and arousing.

Chapter Nineteen

My weaknesses have always been food and men—in that order.
  —Dolly Parton

Guy

I HAVE to willfully pry Scarlett's hand from my leg and hold it tightly in mine because if she keeps touching me, I won't make it to her apartment and I want to get her in a bed, finally.

The ride is silent but buzzing with unspoken anticipation.

Her apartment is a small place in Washington Heights. It's not the best neighborhood, but it's not the worst. At least her building has a front door that locks.

The elevator is broken and we have to take the stairs to the third floor. Walking up the steps behind her is a true exercise in restraint because her jeans hug her form, revealing the shape of her thighs and calves. Calves. I'm turned on by calves. Heaven forbid she reveal an ankle, I might lose my mind.

My already-stretched patience snaps somewhere in the second-floor stairwell and I grab her and push her against the wall, covering her mouth with mine.

Immediately, she moans and lifts a leg around my waist.

Her tongue is in my mouth and my hand is rubbing up the back of her leg and I'm inches from the heat of her when a door slams somewhere and laughter echoes through the space.

She giggles against my mouth and pushes my hand away. "They'll see us. C'mon, hurry."

She grabs my hand and it's a race up the stairs, pounding through the metal handled door, and running along the hallway to her apartment. She fumbles with the key while I nibble on the back of her neck, and then the door opens and we fall inside.

She immediately locks up behind us, then jumps at me. We almost crash to the floor but somehow, I manage to remain standing even while we attack each other with lips and tongues and roaming hands.

Clothes litter the floor around us. I step back, an attempt to slow our frantic movements so I can examine her in the low lights streaming in through the windows.

"Don't move," I whisper the words into her ear, like we're in a church instead of an apartment in Manhattan.

Surprisingly, she listens, and I walk around her slowly, taking my time. With a careful touch, I trace over her shoulder, down her arm, over her stomach, memorizing every part of her with my fingers and leaving a trail of goosebumps in my wake.

Stepping behind her, I press a kiss to where her shoulder meets her neck and trail a line with my lips down her back, pressing a final kiss to her lower back.

Her breathing is erratic. Her hands clench at her sides.

When I slide a hand between her legs from behind, needing to feel how much she wants me, she moans and spreads her legs. I rub her lightly, stroking her slickness while need takes root and grows in my body like an expanding balloon of want. I remove my hand from her before I completely lose it and she spins around, grabbing at me. "Guy, I can't take it anymore. Please."

"Wait." I take both of her hands in mine. "I want to do this in a bed."

"Ugh. Fine, let's go." She yanks me toward the bedroom, all angry kitten and frustrated impatience.

I can't stop laughing. I don't think I've ever laughed so much in one night.

We trip over our clothes in our haste to get to the bedroom. In the darkness, it's mostly a jangle of big lumps. Her bed is unmade and she shoves stuff, clothes I imagine, off the comforter before tugging me down next to her.

"Don't judge me. I'm not as neat as you are. How are you so neat with two teen girls?"

I kiss her shoulder. "I have a maid. She comes twice a month."

"Ah." Her hand runs down my chest, over my stomach, making me suck in a breath, and then she wraps her fingers around the swelling hardness of my erection.

I groan. "Don't worry. It's perfect." I kiss her hard on the mouth and pull back when she slides her hand up and down me. "You're perfect."

"That is a lie." She squeezes me gently and I groan out a laugh.

"Not to me." I lean into her, kissing her ear. "This is a perfect ear." I kiss her collar bone. "This is a perfect collar bone." I shift over her, sliding my tongue down her belly and spreading her knees open.

She sucks in a breath when I blow a heated breath over her exposed flesh.

"This is…definitely perfect."

I start slow, small caresses with my lips, keeping everything light and gentle. I'm in no rush, taking my time, learning what she likes, what makes her squirm and pant and beg for mercy. Until she groans and her hips shift toward me, aching for more. Then I let go. Feasting on her, delighting in the way she moans and clutches at my hair when I hit a sensitive spot. I don't let up until she's finished all over my tongue and then I kiss my way back up her body.

"I want to return the favor," she breathes, grabbing for my pounding erection.

"Later. I need you now. Do you have condoms hiding around here somewhere?" I lift up her pillow in search and she laughs.

"Not here. In the drawer." She rolls over to reach into the nightstand and I run a hand down her backside, enjoying the smoothness of her. She hands me the condom and I slide it on, watching her watch me, biting her lip in anticipation. The move fills me with a sort of caveman satisfaction. But nothing is as satisfying as staring into her eyes as I slide into her. Or when I move slowly in and out, letting the heat build again. Then she's moaning and panting and lifting her hips against me. And when I brush a hand over the space between us and she breaks apart in my arms, forcing me over the edge of the cliff I've been teetering on, I'm convinced. Heaven is here.

Completely sated and spent, she collapses on my chest. I wait until her breathing evens out and slows as sleep claims her, which doesn't take long. I extract myself carefully and make my way to her bathroom to clean up. When I get back to the bed, she's still out. I roll onto the mattress and gently curve around her, following into the warm cocoon of sleep.

I AWAKEN TO TRAFFIC NOISES, honking, brakes screeching, and men yelling. Blinking against brightness, I take in my surroundings. Her room is a mess. Clothing, books, magazines, and makeup strewn haphazardly around the small space, but her bed is comfortable, and her blankets are a tangle of bright colors. It's just like her.

The last thing I want to do is leave the haven of Scarlett's bed, especially when I disentangle myself from her soft, sweet limbs and she makes a cute snuffling sound and rolls over, the sheet lowering to expose her back. Just above her butt, two little dimples wink at me in invitation.

I want nothing more than to spend hours watching

her sleep—the soft curve of her cheek, the delicate part of her lips, her dark red hair spread out like a wave over the pillow—but duty calls.

I get dressed as silently as possible and leave her a note on the kitchen counter before locking up and tapping my phone for an Uber as I head down the stairs.

Then I make a call. "Carson. Have someone deliver a three pack of the chocolate croissants and an Americano with cream and sugar to this address." I rattle off. "Apartment 309. Make sure they deliver it by eight."

A beat of silence and then, "Is that Scarlett's apartment?"

"None of your business."

"You know I'll find out."

"Then why bother asking? I'll be there in a couple of hours."

I hang up on him, a smile tugging at my lips. I think I have the inklings of a solution to Scarlett keeping her spot. I kind of like having her across the street and in close proximity. Maybe I could get some blinds for my office so we could…. I shake the thought away before I devolve into a Neanderthal.

One thing at a time. The first item on my agenda is taking my ideas and formulating an actual plan on paper. Something I can show Oliver to get him on board.

He doesn't like change. I know it will be a hard sell, but hope fills me with purpose.

This has to work.

I get home in time to see the girls before they head off to school. Ava makes us scrambled eggs and toast which is about the limit of her culinary abilities. We eat at the table together and I get a text from Scarlett to thank me for the croissants and coffee accompanied by lots of heart eye emojis that make me grin like a loon.

Then Emma reaches out to try and flip my lip with a finger and I laugh and dodge her attempts at physical comedy.

I walk the girls out to their ride to school. Most of the time I drive them, but I don't have time this morning, so I called up one of my drivers.

As we're hugging goodbye, Emma pats me on the cheek and holds up her phone.

It's a video of me, earlier, smiling at Scarlett's text, my eyes are bright, and I have…is that a dimple? I'm so happy. Surprised, I meet Emma's eyes, but she's already turned away, getting into the car with her sister's help.

I watch the car drive away and shake my head. That kid.

It's time to get to work.

"Carson. My office, now. Bring your laptop," I tell him as I'm walking past his desk and into the office.

We spend over an hour, hashing out the idea, bouncing ideas around. Finally, we have something in place that might work.

"We need to contact Roger right away. I bet Crawford and Company will take this deal. You'll just need to talk to Bethany Connell and explain things."

I nod. "Should we tell Oliver first? My inclination is to wait until it's more or less a done deal."

Carson considers the question for a second and then dips his head. "I agree. It is probably better to beg forgiveness than to ask permission he probably won't give, anyway."

"Make the call."

He walks out to his desk and excitement thrums through me. I can't wait to tell Scarlett, but I need to hold off until I make sure it can actually work. There are a few pieces that still need to be tied together, and Oliver is one of them.

A few minutes later, Carson is at the door. "Boss? We got a little problem."

"What is it?"

"I talked to Roger and, well, the deal was already done."

My face goes slack. "How is that possible?"

"I guess Oliver—"

"Get him on the phone," I bark. "Now."

I take a deep breath. Dammit. I should have known Oliver would go behind my back. There's no way it could be finalized yet, though. I haven't signed any papers and we're in this together and he wouldn't go that far. Would he?

"I got Oliver."

I put it on speaker and he immediately starts talking. "Before you say anything, you're welcome."

"For what?"

"Marie signed your divorce papers. I had them couriered over to your attorney this morning."

"That's…thank you, but—"

"And I got Crawford and Company to sell that little piece of real estate we've been waiting on, so we can sign in two weeks and we can move forward with our plans."

I have to tread carefully, here. "That's great, Oliver, and I have some ideas for what we could do with the lot. You know how we had talked about guest chef nights? We could expand the concept outdoors with various food trucks. Give them a time slot to rent, it will generate additional income streams and we'll give our customers a food experience with real variety."

He's quiet for a second and then, "That's a great idea."

I let out a breath.

"I love it. Now you just have to get rid of the cupcake lady."

So close.

"About that—"

"Guy." His voice is as sharp as my best blade. "If you open your mouth and tell me you're letting her stay there, you've lost it. This idea could work, but if she moves, we could fit more variety in there and make twice as much. If you tell me you're changing all of our plans simply because you're fucking the cupcake woman, I don't care how cute she is, you've been compromised and this whole thing will be a disaster." His voice escalates as he speaks.

I think quickly. This is classic Oliver. He'll huff and puff and then later he'll think about it; I'll give him more reasons to think about it, and I'll eventually talk him down to my side. It just might not be as easy as I'd like. But when has anything in my life been easy?

"Fine. It's not important. Just do what you need to, get the deal done, and we'll talk after."

I hang up right as there is a tap at the door.

It's Scarlett. "How could you?"

Chapter Twenty

IF MORE OF US VALUED FOOD AND CHEER AND SONG ABOVE hoarded gold, it would be a merrier world.
    —J.R.R. Tolkien

Scarlett

WHAT STARTED out as the best day in my life sure turned into a shit show real quick.

It started early. We had barely started serving the lunch crowd when Fred called out to me.

"Scarlett, someone is here to see you."

"Is it Guy?"

"Nope."

I move toward her to glance out the order window.

It's definitely not Guy. It's Marie.

She's wearing big sunglasses and a large fur coat.

"I'll meet you in the back." I point.

She nods and her heels clickety clack to the back of the truck.

"You know the diva?" Fred asks.

"It's Guy's ex."

Her lips twist. "Yikes."

"Something like that."

I brace myself, and then open the back door and step out onto the sidewalk. "Can I help you?"

"Look, I know I was a total bitch the other night, but I wanted to warn you."

Oh boy. I relax a little. This is classic school yard nonsense. Guy was her shiny toy she didn't want, but now that someone else has him and he's happy, she wants the toy back.

I decide right away I won't believe anything she says, no matter how convincing she is.

"Oh?" I feign interest.

"I thought you should know, from one woman to another. He acts like he's for real, but he's a user. All men are. He always says I'm manipulative, and I guess I can be, but he's the real mastermind and I don't want you to fall into his trap." She sniffs and a delicately manicured hand slides a perfectly pressed handkerchief from her pocket, and she dabs it under her sunglasses.

I want to laugh, but I manage to suppress the urge. "You're good. I'll give you that."

She steps toward me and lifts the sunglasses to the top of her head.

I lean back, her appearance giving me a start. Her

eyes are rimmed and red. She's close enough that it's obvious the grey smudges under her eyes are not a product of makeup or some kind of trickery. You can't fake that level of exhaustion.

"I know that I messed up when I left Guy. I knew it right away. I've spent the last year wondering if I could return and pick things up like they were. But the thing is, if you want to be with him, you have to accept that he'll always put you last. His sisters and his business, and basically everything else will come first. He doesn't really care about anyone but himself."

I search her eyes. She's being sincere, I think. But this whole conversation is odd.

She pulls her shades down and slips the handkerchief back into her pocket with a shrug. "Anyway, to prove my point, he's already bought this property. So, you aren't any different from me, really. He was using you until the deal went through." She waves a hand around. "You can go ask him if you don't believe me. I'm just trying to do the right thing."

And she walks away, unconcerned.

I watch her go, and the old niggle of doubt intrudes. The one I thought Guy had banished forever, especially after last night and then this morning. I mean, he had someone bring me coffee. He left me a note about how much he enjoyed last night and he drew little silly stick figures in compromising positions. He cares about me. It wasn't some elaborate hoax, there would be no reason for it.

I won't call him in a panic. I won't be someone who

freaks out over nothing. I can get an answer to this very quickly and I won't even have to see Guy to do it.

I call Bethany.

"Hello friend!" Bethany yells into my ear.

"Aren't you at work?"

"Yeah," she snorts, "I just freaked out my assistant. Sorry Todd!"

"Hey, quick question. Did Crawford and Company sell the lot where I'm parked?"

"No way."

I knew it.

"But actually, I don't know. I don't think so. Let me double check for you, hold please."

She puts me on hold and I listen to elevator music for about thirty seconds.

"Shit, Scarlett," she says as soon as she clicks back onto the line.

My stomach drops to my toes.

No. No no no. It's not true. It can't be.

Black spots swim across my field of vision and I sit on the bumper of the truck and take deep breaths.

Bethany is still talking in my ear. Something about how the deal is final, but papers haven't been signed, yet, everything still has to go through escrow. But I barely hear her. I feel sick. But maybe still, there's something going on. He can explain it. I know it.

After everything we've done and everything he said, he wouldn't do this to me, not without some kind of plan, like he said. But then why didn't he tell me?

But the little voices in my head are buzzing in a chorus

of "I told you so's" because I always do this. I always believe in love and forever after and every time it's a lie. Past experience is waving a red flag and telling me I'm the biggest moron in the history of idiots.

I don't even know if I say goodbye to Bethany. Somehow, she's not on the line anymore and I walk across the street in a daze.

"Scarlett?" Fred calls out behind me from the order window. "What's going on?"

But I keep walking. Carson isn't at his desk. I stop outside Guy's office and the words hit me like bullets in my chest.

"If you tell me you're changing all of our plans simply because you're fucking the cupcake woman, I don't care how cute she is, you've been compromised and this whole thing will be a disaster."

And then Guy's response. ""Fine. It's not important. Just do what you need to, get the deal done, and we'll talk after."

I can't breathe. This isn't happening to me. Again.

"Guy?"

"Scarlett." His eyes drop. Guiltily.

"You...you bought the...you did it. That thing you said you weren't going to do." I can't even say it.

And now here I am staring into those stark green eyes. Confusion pierces into the fog of emotions roiling through me. He does appear sincerely contrite. His brows are down.

He walks around his desk to approach me, hands out.

"I didn't know—"

"You didn't know? You said it's not important when that…man said you were fucking the cupcake woman."

He winces. "Oliver is a dick. And that's not what I meant."

I want to believe him. I want it so bad I can taste it. But all my old insecurities and doubts are banging against my ribs, harder than my heart is pounding, beating me up from the inside out. I always make bad decisions with men. And this was a colossal mistake, from the beginning, and this time I knew it. And still, I thought, once again, that I would be enough to make someone care. I was wrong.

"Well it meant something to me. And now it means we're done." My voice cracks on the last work, but it doesn't affect him.

The shutters fall over his eyes. He steps back, face impassive, the old emotionless mask I once knew. "You haven't even let me explain. You're really going to let this get between us?" The words aren't a plea for forgiveness, they're remote. Cold. He really doesn't care.

No one ever does. How could I have expected more?

"I didn't let anything get between us. You did," I say.

"I told you I would find a mutually beneficial solution and I still intend to."

How can I believe him? His other words are still ringing in my head. *Not important.*

I can't stand here and gaze at his beautiful, distant face. It's too much. And so, I do the thing I've been trying not to do all along.

I run.

GETTING TO BLUE FALLS, Texas from New York is quite a trip. All I could afford was a terrible flight on the worst airline ever with no snacks and three layovers on Christmas Day. And that's not even the end, because once I got to the airport, I had to rent a car and drive an hour to get home. We're only staying two days, including today, so in forty-eight hours we get to fly home in misery again.

Bah humbug.

"I'm so glad we're both alone on Christmas."

To top it all off, I have had to listen to Fred talk the entire time.

"We aren't alone," I say.

"I mean, we have each other. You're right, I shouldn't negate that. And our families. But you know, we don't have men anymore. If this was, like Regency England, we would be total old spinster maids. On the shelf. Long in the tooth. Did you know, the phrase originally derived from horses? Their teeth never stop growing."

I sigh and tune her out.

It's been a week since I last saw Guy.

He tried to call me. Once. I didn't answer, and he hasn't tried again.

I haven't been parking next to his restaurant, even though I could. I had some last-minute catering gigs before the holidays to take care of, which I did from my home and the commissary. I've spent a lot of time with Fred's family, eating terrible vegan food and absorbing the warmth of a loving family like it might jolt me back to my former self.

But I don't know if former Scarlett is ever coming back. It's like a change in the Gregorian Calendar. There's Before Guy and After Guy. But…whatever that would be in Latin. Fred's family is really rubbing off on me.

At least now, I'll get to see my actual family. I'm excited, but also exhausted and drained, wrung out like an old dish rag.

Pulling up the gravel drive, memories flood me. Images flickering in my mind like an old timey video. Riding bikes down the lane with Reese—who I would make bundle up in a helmet, knee pads, elbow pads, and any other kind of pad I could find. Playing in the sprinkler in the grass in the front yard. Granny yelling at us to wash our hands after catching toads in the pond over yonder, behind the house.

I can't believe it's been two years. I stop and stare up at the familiar, colorful monstrosity of my childhood home.

"Wow," Fred says. "Are those shutters orange?"

"Yes." I try to see the house from a stranger's viewpoint, but I can't. Yes, it's colorful and kind of weird, from the bright yellow rocking chair on the porch to the red trim and blue shingles. But to me it's just home.

I vaguely wonder what my parents are doing but then realize I don't care. They aren't really my family, not like Reese and Granny and…like I thought Guy would be. The family you choose.

The front door swings open and Reese comes running out, her smile so big it lights up the whole laneway. She's wearing Christmas pajamas and a headband with reindeer antlers and they jiggle on her head as she runs toward me.

I open the car door and slide out to meet her halfway.

"Scarlett!" She throws herself into my arms and then we're hugging like it's been twenty years instead of two. "You're here! We made pie," she tells me.

And that's when I burst into tears.

"Oh, dear." Reese pats me on the back. "Are you okay?"

"Do I need to shoot someone?" Granny asks from behind her.

"No, no, it's fine." I wipe at my eyes and peek over Reese's shoulder at Granny. She's wearing a vibrant rainbow scarf around her neck over her own red and green long johns. And she's not alone. There's a whole crowd of people on the porch behind her, all wearing Christmas pajamas and watching the exchange with curiosity.

"Howdy y'all! I'm Fred," Fred calls out from behind me.

I laugh wetly into Reese's shoulder. "Fred, people don't really talk like that here."

"We sure as shit do," Granny says. "Come on in, y'all, it's getting mighty chilly out here. Beast made up some hot cocoa and it will keep you warm so you can explain why you've become a watering pot." She turns away, mumbling under her breath, "Damn city folk probably ruined you for life." Then louder, "Beast! Get out extra moonshine!" She leads us up to the porch and into the house.

Once we're crowded in the kitchen, Reese introduces

everyone, but I can't quite focus on all the names she's throwing out. Fitz is her boyfriend, so I keep that one close, but then there's also his sister Annabel, her boyfriend Jude, and then Jude's sister and brother—this part of the introduction gets convoluted because apparently, they're all sort of siblings, but not really—Beast and Grace.

Beast hands me a steaming mug during this whole process.

"Thank you," I tell him, taking a long sip. Extra moonshine cocoa. I sure have missed Granny.

He gets Fred a cup, too and she doesn't even thank him, just stares up at him like he might eat her. He's a hulking mess of a man, with dark hair and inscrutable expression. Wide as a house.

He takes up position by the door while the rest of us are crowded around the kitchen.

"Tell me who I have to kill or maim or both," Granny insists.

I glance around uncomfortably at the assembled crowd, and thankfully, Jude takes the hint.

"Why don't we go pick out a Christmas movie for everyone to watch?" he says, rubbing his beard.

"I get to pick first!" Grace, his sort-of sister—a small wisp of a blonde who can't be more than thirteen—scrambles out to the living room, sliding on the hardwood in her socks.

Jude and Annabel follow her, along with a rambling Beast. Fitz kisses Reese on the cheek and exits to the living room, offering me a handsome smile on his way out.

And then finally, Fred. "I've heard this story a thousand times," she rolls her eyes, but then squeezes my shoulder before disappearing after the others.

Now it's me and Granny and Reese. I take another sip of my spiked cocoa and scan Reese. Really getting an eyeful. She looks so happy. I mean, right now, she's got a crease between her brows and she's frowning at me with concern, but I can still see the change in her. Her whole stature is straight and open, not like she was before where it was like she was always trying to hide herself. The guilt I had felt for leaving her washes away now that I can witness her transformation with my own eyes. From cater-pillar to butterfly.

I grab her hand. "I'm so happy you found your tribe. I can't wait to get to know them more."

"Me, too." She squeezes my fingers. "But tell us what's going on. Why all the tears?"

"I don't know where to start."

"I do," Granny says. She leans back and takes a sip out of her mug with a smirk. "It was the brooch, just like I told you."

I gasp and then gape at her. "It *was* the brooch."

Reese glances between us, a crease between her brows. "What?"

I fill them both in, starting with the night of the charity event, explaining everything that happened, including bits of what had gone before with the fire inci-dent. I skim over the sexy bits, but they get the gist, anyway.

Toward the end, when I explain what I overheard, Granny stops me. "Eavesdroppers never hear anything good of themselves. And eavesdropping is a dick move."

"Granny!"

"I'm telling you, girl, you should have let him explain."

"It wasn't like that," I defend myself. "I was going to let him explain and then I heard the conversation. Besides, he didn't want to explain."

She puffs out a short laugh. "Of course not, not after you were ready to bolt at the first sign of conflict."

I'm shocked into silence.

"I didn't bolt at the first sign of conflict. There was the whole, oh yeah, I'm married thing, too."

"He explained that, and you forgave him."

"And?"

Granny taps my hand. "You can't keep bringing it up if it's forgiven. That's not fair. You want to believe he's like that Bruce Conway, but he's not."

I bite my lip. Is she right?

Reese takes a more diplomatic approach. "He said he was working on something else, right?"

"Yes, but I don't know what it was. He never bothered telling me."

Reese and Granny exchange a glance.

"You're supposed to be on my side!"

"We are on your side," Reese says. "Why don't you just talk to him? And let him explain everything?"

My eyes fall shut and I lean forward, head in hands. "I've waited too long. He won't talk to me."

"You have to at least try," Reese says. "Worst case scenario, you're right, and then you will have lost nothing."

Nerves flutter in my belly at the thought of reaching

out to Guy. I don't know if I could handle it if he gave me the cold shoulder or dismissed me out of hand.

Not to mention the one thing I should be more concerned about: my business and what I'm going to do with For Goodness Cakes after the holidays. What if it fails?

"What if I have to close down the truck?"

"No," Reese's denial is instantaneous. "You'll think of something. You always do."

Granny puts her hand over mine. "Every storm runs out of rain."

"What if I'm too afraid to even get wet?"

Granny shakes her head. "You got soaked the second you walked out of this town and didn't look back. The problem is you're afraid of failure, but the real fear should be regret. You won't fail. You can't because you have everything you need inside you, and no one can take that away unless you let them."

I blink at her. It's like Guy said, I am enough. And they're both right. I will find somewhere else to sell my cakes and make people smile. I will continue to grow my catering business. This isn't the end, it's the beginning.

Granny continues, "And you should listen to me because I'm old and ornery and if you don't, I might shoot you."

Reese and I laugh, but Granny doesn't.

"Come on," I stand up. "You've listened to me whine and complain long enough. Let's go join the others."

But I don't go into the living room right away. They go, and I stay in the kitchen and try to call Guy before I chicken out.

The call goes straight to voicemail. I hang up without leaving a message. This doesn't feel like something I want to get into with a recording. I power my phone off. I don't want to be distracted when there's not much I can do about the Guy situation. I'll enjoy the limited time with my family and worry about Guy when I get back to New York tomorrow.

Chapter Twenty-One

HE WHO EATS ALONE CHOKES ALONE.
 – Arabian Proverb

Guy

CHRISTMAS IS one of my favorite days of the year. Not so much because I enjoy it myself, but because there is nothing like witnessing the joy and wonder of Christmas through a child's eyes.

Emma pokes me in the cheek and lifts her iPad for me to see the display. She's brought up pictures of breakfast with Santa at Rockefeller Center from last year. It's a tradition.

"We're leaving soon," I tell her. I booked us for the 8:15 time slot, knowing we would be up early already. Neither of the girls can contain their excitement over the holidays. They woke me up at five this morning, jumping on my bed and laughing with eagerness.

They've finished opening all their presents and watching them shriek with glee at their gifts fills my chest with the glow of happiness. It's almost enough to fill up the hole in my heart, but not quite.

I bought her a gift last week. It's just a silly little thing, an apron that says, *Don't be afraid to take whisks*. It's still under the tree.

After showing me the pictures of Santa last year, Emma scrambles off the couch, grabs Scarlett's present and chucks it at me. The toss goes wide, but I manage to catch it.

She can't know who it's for. Can she? The girls only met Scarlett a couple of times. Then again, it's not like I bring strangers around. Ever.

I set the present on the coffee table.

Emma comes back next to me on the couch and holds up her iPad again. This time, it's the video she took of me after my night with Scarlett.

The man in the video grins at his phone like a lovesick fool.

If only he knew. The pain of witnessing my own previous happiness lances through me like a sword in the gut. But I've always known the truth, life isn't about being happy. It's about being responsible.

If I had only focused on my responsibilities, maybe none of this would have happened.

But then I remember Scarlett—her smell, the way she moves, the way she laughs at herself, the way she takes care of everyone around her and spreads happiness like it's necessity and not a luxury.

I miss her. The lack of her smile is an ever-present ache in my chest.

I should have fought harder, but the way she was so willing to throw it all away reminded me that love and happiness have never been something within my reach.

But what if it was? What if it still is?

"I know, Emma. I get it. Come on, let's get ready for Santa."

Ava helps me get Emma dressed and ready as much as we can manage. Emma is in a goofy mood, grabbing the brush away, poking me in the ear and laughing, and pulling at Ava's hair, but eventually we are ready to go down to the car.

Breakfast with Santa should be perfect. Two little elves take the girls to meet Santa in the throne room. They get a toy and a personalized ornament. The food is good, brioche French toast, scrambled eggs, pastries and ginger-bread men. The setting can't be better, we're flanked by glittery angel sculptures and in view of the famous Rocke-feller Center Christmas tree.

But the whole time, even though I put on a brave face, I'm miserable. I've been miserable. I don't know what to do with myself. But I also don't know how to fix the problem.

When we get home, I put on Mr. Bean in the hopes the girls will sit still long enough to let the food settle before we go swimming.

And then I turn on my phone to check my messages. Nothing.

On the TV, Mr. Bean is at the pool. He's hanging onto the side of the diving platform for dear life, his brows lifted, eyes wide, lips twitching in terror.

I can relate.

My phone rings and I tug it out of my pocket.

Oliver.

On Christmas? Really? He probably has no idea what day it is. I leave the girls on the couch and walk into the next room.

"What?" I answer.

What happened with Scarlett wasn't entirely his fault, but I still have the urge to punch him in the face.

"Why is Emma sending me pictures of you looking like someone kicked your puppy?"

Apparently, my brave face isn't so brave, after all.

"That's none of your business."

He sighs. "I know you're pissed at me, but I do care about your welfare."

I laugh. "Because I'm the one doing all the work for our project."

"A project funded almost entirely by me."

I shake my head at the reminder. "With my name bringing in the customers." Damn him. If this whole thing fails, he'll be out nothing. It's chump change to him. In his world, this is all a game and the people are just chess pieces.

I can't do this anymore.

"I want to change the deal," I say.

"Guy. We've talked about this." His tone is calm and condescending, like he's talking to a recalcitrant child.

"No. You've talked about this. Now it's my turn. I'll

sign the papers on the real estate, except for the north corner. Large enough for a food truck. If you don't agree, I'm cutting my losses and pulling out of this *partnership*." I say partnership like it's a dirty word.

"You're bluffing. You can't do that. We've signed contracts. I'll—"

I hang up on him.

Relief floods through my body in a wave.

This isn't all about Scarlett, it's about so much more. It's about not being under Oliver's thumb. This partnership won't work out in the long run if Oliver makes all our decisions, runs rough shod over anything I want to do and throws his financial backing in my face as a means of control.

The project is doomed if we continue on like we have been.

In the end, it's about being happy. Yes, I want Scarlett in my life and I will do anything to get her back, if she'll still have me.

But I'll kill this deal regardless. Either way, she wins.

I might learn how to be happy, eventually, without Scarlett in my life. My days would go on without her. But I want her in it, and if there is any way to make it happen, I'm going for it.

Emma ambles in from the living room and reaches for me, giving me a hug with her jerky gait that's half-violent in its intensity.

She shows me her iPad again, while hanging on to my arm. It's a selfie of her and Scarlett they must have taken when she was here for dinner. Emma's expression is very serious, and she's focused on something to the side. Scarlett is smiling into the camera, her happy face sending sparks of longing through me. The craving to see her, touch her, make her smile, pounds through me like a physical ache.

"I know," I tell Emma. "I'll get her back."

IT TAKES a while for me to find Granny's address in Blue Falls, Texas.

It's going to take even longer to actually get there. But Oliver, surprisingly, helps.

"Okay, look," he says when he shows up at my apartment, unannounced, the day after Christmas. The day after I ignored all his calls. "I know I'm an asshole. You win. Your fuckable cupcake lady can keep her little section, but that's it, you don't get anything else from me."

"Oliver," I cut him off with a sharp tone and then point at the girls on the couch.

Emma waves two hands at him, and Ava's eyes are wide, brows up.

"Sorry for the language, ladies." He lifts his hands in apology.

I rub my chin. "I'll forgive you if you let me borrow your private jet."

His hands come up again, this time in defense. "Woah, woah, woah, there, settle down Casanova. Why do you need my plane?"

"He's going to get Scarlett back!" Ava yells. "It's so romantic."

Oliver grimaces.

"And you can stay here and watch the girls," I tell him.

His eyes widen in panic. "No way. I'll take Emma, but that's it."

"What?" Ava protests. "What about me?"

"Sorry. It's just, you talk too much."

"I was kidding." I shake my head. "Clara is coming over in the morning to stay with them."

He sighs. "Good. *We* can take my plane." Then he grins at me.

I groan. "Fine. I guess I'll let you come with me on your plane."

I can't believe he agreed at all, to be honest.

I've never flown on a private jet before and I'm not sure I could ever go back to first class. It's efficient and quiet and comfortable and spacious. Sleek gray leather seats, no crowds, and actual decent food.

"Here." Oliver taps on his cell and leans over the wide space between us to show me. "You can download an app to adjust the window tint and temperature and whatever you want to watch." He gestures to the flat screen on the wall.

I shake my head. "You see Oliver, this is why you're a dick."

He shoves a bite of beluga caviar in his mouth and washes it down with champagne. "What do you mean?" His expression is the picture of innocence.

We land at the private airstrip and still have to drive almost an hour to get to the house. Oliver makes me drive. He probably doesn't even know how.

The last leg of the trip is never-ending. When we're finally cruising down a long gravel driveway, my heart is thumping, my palms are sweaty, and I start to wonder if I'm making a huge mistake and she's going to tell me to go to hell.

"You look like you're gonna spew," Oliver says.

"Thanks for the vote of confidence."

He shrugs.

The car comes to a stop and we exit the vehicle, stretching our limbs.

It's a sprawling ranch-style home with orange shutters, red trim, blue shingles, and a vivid yellow rocking chair on the porch.

We jog up the front steps to the door. There's a shotgun leaning up against the wall. Is that even legal?

I lift a hand to knock and before my knuckles can hit the wood, it swings open. At the door is an elderly woman with long gray braids, red overalls, and an antique wood pipe in her mouth.

"Gentlemen," she greets us, talking around the lip of the pipe. A stream of bubbles blows out the bowl. She whoops and Oliver flinches next to me, startled by the piercing sound propelled from the little old lady.

"Granny?" I ask.

She cocks her head at me. "Are you a long-lost grandchild?"

"No. I'm trying to find Scarlett."

Her eyes flash between me and Oliver and then narrow back on me. "Are you, now?"

"Is she here?"

She sighs and steps back. "I reckon y'all better come in."

Fifteen minutes later, I'm helping Granny change a

light bulb in the foyer, while Oliver dusts a fan in the living room.

I'm not even really sure how this all came about. I had begun to explain why I was there, but then Granny went off about her rheumatism and the next thing I knew, we were helping her with chores. I still don't even know if Scarlett is in the house somewhere, but I doubt it. It's too quiet.

"That's mighty kind of you," Granny tells me when I'm stepping down from the short ladder she had set up for me to reach the recessed lighting.

"Can we talk about Scarlett now?" I ask.

"I suppose it's time. Come on into the kitchen, I made some sweet tea."

I follow her into the open concept kitchen. There are high ceilings in here, too, along with top of the line stainless steel appliances, a double stove, and dark granite countertops.

I'm impressed.

She hands me a glass of tea. I thank her absently and take a sip.

Damn, that's more than sweet. I have to work to contain my initial, mouth-twisting reaction to the sugar content.

And then I notice the shotgun from the porch is propped against the counter, within reaching distance.

Not my reaching distance. Hers.

"What are your intentions with my granddaughter?" Gone is the whimsical little old lady with the bubble pipe, and in her place is someone who might actually murder me.

"Did I mention I brought you a gift?"

One slender brow lifts and she crosses her arms over her chest. "Did you now?"

"Some champagne. I left it in the car." Hijacked from Oliver's plane. Thank God I had the foresight to grab it. I knew meeting Scarlett's family for the first time necessitated some kind of gift. My parents taught me that much.

She purses her lips and nods at me. "You can get it later. For now, answer the question, young man."

"My intentions . . ." I sigh and scrub a hand through my hair. "I want to make her smile," I say finally.

She stares at me in stony silence for a few long seconds and then she grins. "That's a good answer. A damn good answer. Go get the champagne, my boy."

I nod and run out to the car. When I come back, Oliver is in the kitchen, sitting on a stool and grimacing at his own cup of sweet tea.

"Did you get the fans dusted?" I ask, enjoying the fact that Oliver had to participate in some kind of manual labor, probably for the first time in his life. I put the champagne in the fridge.

"I did. They actually weren't very dusty."

"It's possible I had someone over earlier this week for cleaning before the holidays," Granny reveals nonchalantly. "I had a boyfriend named Oliver once," she adds.

"Did you now?" I ask.

"He was terrible in bed."

Oliver chokes on his tea and I bark out a laugh.

"Where is Scarlett?" I ask.

Granny sighs. "She's on her way back from the airport."

My heart skips a beat and then resumes course, triple time. "She is?"

"She left this morning to head back to the city. But she sent a message before you pulled up. She was already on her way back because her flight was cancelled. She and that Fred girl should be here any minute."

Gravel crunches outside. Without another word, I sprint to the front door.

Chapter Twenty-Two

COOKING IS LIKE LOVE. IT SHOULD BE ENTERED INTO WITH abandon or not at all.
    —Harriet Van Horne

Scarlett

"YOU KNOW, this is like a sign. We should stay here forever and not go back to New York."

I shake my head. "That's not going to work for me."

We drive in silence for a few minutes, and then Fred pipes up again.

"Did you try calling?"

I know what she's asking without having to clarify. I've been moping about Guy since we got here Christmas morning. "I did before we left the airport. It rang, but he didn't answer." I put on the turn signal to head north from

Main Street in the heart of Blue Falls. We'll be back at the ranch within ten minutes.

"He's probably busy with his sisters."

I appreciate that she's trying to make me feel better, but it's not working.

"Maybe."

Or maybe he's avoiding you, the insidious little voice whispers inside me. Why did I let everything get to me? Why did I run, again? I've been making one-sided bargains to the universe all morning that I won't run anymore, if only I can get back to New York and track Guy down.

The airport was a nightmare. Packed with travelers. We got stuck in line at security while someone coughed behind us like they were carrying the plague, and even after all that our flight was cancelled due to a blizzard in the city.

At least I'll get to spend more time with my family. The only bright spot in this terrible week.

We rumble down the long driveway and as the house comes into view, so does an unfamiliar car out front.

"Who's that?" Fred asks.

"I have no idea." I don't recognize the black town car.

Before we've even come to a full stop, a tall figure emerges from the front door and jogs down the steps.

"Is that—?"

Fred hasn't even finished her sentence and I've fumbled out of my seat belt and leapt out of the car like it's on fire.

I only make it two steps, and then he's there, showing no signs of slowing.

"What are you—?"

His arms surround me, strong bands of comfort, and his mouth crashes down on mine.

I'm not complaining. I kiss him back, wrapping my arms around his waist, pressing my body to his. A mixture of emotions swirls like soup in the pot of my body: shock that he's here, joy, relief, undying gratitude. It's really him. He's really here and he's really kissing me. I don't want to let him go, afraid if I do, he'll disappear, and this will all be some kind of surreal dream.

Some time passes before he pulls back and then rests his forehead against mine.

"Hi," he says between breaths.

"Hi."

He swallows. "I'm sorry."

"No, I'm sorry. I should have listened to you. I overreacted, and then I panicked, and I ruined everything."

"No. I shouldn't have been dismissive of you, even if it was just to get Oliver off my back."

"No, I should have—"

"We get it," Fred calls out, walking in a wide circle around us to reach the house. "You're both morons."

Granny is on the porch and she ushers Fred inside. "I'm glad you're here. I need your help . . ."

They disappear and then it's only the two of us out in the chilled December air.

"How did you get here?" I ask him.

"Oliver's private plane."

My eyes widen. "Seriously?"

"Yeah. I sort of threatened to quit the restaurant project."

Astonishment has me jerking back to back to stare up

into his face. "Seriously? You shouldn't have done that for me."

He rubs his hands up and down my arms. "It wasn't entirely for you. You were the impetus that made me realize it wouldn't work with Oliver. Not if it continued like it was. Oliver was using his financial backing as a means to make him the dictator of our business decisions. And I was letting him. If I hadn't stood my ground, the relationship would have become toxic and it wouldn't have worked out, anyway. Really, you saved me from making a terrible decision."

"Wow. But after that, he let you use his plane?"

He smiles, the dimple in his cheek making an appearance. "He came with me. And he agreed to leave a portion of the real estate to Crawford and Company so your deal with them can continue and you won't feel beholden to me or Oliver for renting it."

"That's amazing." I can't believe he did it. He really did it, just like he promised. I should have trusted him all along.

"There's more." His eyes move from mine, one hand coming up to rub a strand of my hair between his fingers. "We're going to rent out the other portion of the lot, on a rotational basis. We already planned to have guest chef nights at both restaurants, and this way we can have a variety of options for outdoor venues, too. I want your help with that part, though."

"You do?"

"Maybe you could help me vet some of the trucks?"

My mouth is hanging open. I snap it shut. "Of course."

His shoulders drop, sudden tension releasing from them. "Good."

"There's only one more thing we have to resolve, then."

His eyes search mine. "What is it?"

"If our weird really matches."

He lets out a bark of laughter, his head falling back. "Oh, it definitely does."

"How can you be so sure?"

His hand comes up the back of my neck, tangling in my hair and tugging my head back gently. He presses closer. Our mouths are inches apart.

"I'm not perfect," he says.

I gasp in feigned shock.

"And neither are you."

"Hey."

He smiles, a brilliant flash that momentarily blinds me. "You'll be the spotlight that helps me find and smooth all my jagged edges and bad behaviors. I'll keep you safe and supported when you feel the urge to flee. I might even rescue you if you ever get caught on a doorknob, in a chandelier, or a . . ." He shrugs. "Giant sombrero."

I laugh.

He continues. "Together, we are better than perfect. We're two flawed humans who care about each other."

I blink back tears. "You might be right."

He leans in, but instead of kissing me like I want, he slides against me so our cheeks are pressed together. Then he whispers in my ear, "I love you."

The tears are leaking out now. I couldn't stop them if I tried.

"I love you, too."

Then he's kissing my tears and the only place I ever want to hide again is in the shelter of his arms.

"Y'all about done out here?" Granny calls out. "I could use some help feeding the chickens before dinner."

I lean around Guy. Granny's on the front porch, watching us with a pipe in her mouth.

Guy and I exchange a smile, then hand in hand, we head up to the house.

"You've got a Michelin-rated chef at your disposal and you want him to feed the chickens?" I ask.

"We don't need any of that highfalutin' food around here. My brisket is better than anything you're gonna find in those fancy city places. And if you young folk think you're sharing a bed under my roof before you're married, you better think again," she grumbles.

Guy pulls me close, whispering in my ear, "I'll sneak into your room later."

"I'm counting on it," I whisper back.

He leans in again. "I brought condoms for you to hide wherever you want."

I laugh so hard I almost run into the wall.

Yep. Perfect.

THE END

Epilogue

ALL YOU NEED IS LOVE. BUT A LITTLE CHOCOLATE NOW AND then doesn't hurt.

   —Charles M. Schulz

I MIGHT BE DREAMING.

The murmur of sounds reaches me from a distance: voices, birds, wind blowing through trees. I'm vaguely aware of the shifting of a body next to me. The warmth of sunlight on my face. A soft blanket under my back. My stomach is full. The air is warm and scented with trees and Guy's pine-scented cologne.

"Don't go too far. Stay where I can see you," Guy's voice calls, near my head.

The warm length of his arm settles around my midsection.

His voice tickles my ear. "Are you sleeping?"

"Yes. But no dream has ever been this good."

"What are you dreaming about?"

I turn into him, hiding my face in the crook of his neck. "We're having a picnic in Central Park. On Great Hill. Near the trees. The girls are playing with bubbles and I'm lying on a blanket with you. It's a sunny, beautiful day and I have everything I could ever want."

His lips brush my hair. "It's not a dream."

"Thank God." I lift my head and his mouth presses to mine.

"Ew!" Ava shrieks from somewhere nearby.

We turn toward the noise. Both girls are standing about ten feet away from our picnic spread. Ava's got her eyes pressed shut. Emma is next to her, grinning. She smacks the bubble stick out of Ava's hand.

"Emma!" They run off into spring sunshine.

Guy's arms tighten around me, his eyes meet mine, the green hue lightened by the sun, matching the grass around us. "I was going to ask you—"

His phone rings. He curses but doesn't let go of me, only removes one arm and wiggles to excavate the phone out of his pocket before pressing it to his ear. "This better be an emergency," he answers.

Carson's voice is a murmur on the other end of the line.

I snuggle deeper into Guy's side and his free arm squeezes me gently.

"Okay. Right. Sounds good. That's all fine. Now don't bother me for another hour."

Carson responds, but all I can make out is a distant "waa waa waa", like he's one of the adults on *Charlie Brown*.

"I don't care if the restaurant catches fire—okay fine, call me if someone's dying, otherwise, I'll be in later."

He hangs up without another word and tosses his phone. Then both his arms surround me.

"What did Carson want?" I ask into his t-shirt.

"To tell me the divorce was finalized."

I lift my head. "Really?"

He smiles, the dimple appears, and I wonder if I'm dreaming again. "Really."

"Hmm. Good."

I snuggle back in. "I feel bad for her."

"Me too."

Four months ago, I wouldn't have conceived of being so magnanimous. After our little conversation, I thought Marie would do her best to continually make life hell for Guy, and therefore me, by proxy. But instead, she more than cooperated. She even apologized, in person, first to Guy and then to me. She seemed legitimately sincere—not a crocodile tear in sight. She said she has abandonment issues that have nothing to do with Guy or anyone else, and everything to do with how she perceives herself.

"Can we have ice cream?" Ava is back, at the edge of the blanket now.

"In a minute," Guy says.

Ava groans and flits away with Emma again.

Wasn't Guy going to ask me something? "What were you going to—?" My phone rings, vibrating in my back pocket.

Guy groans and slides his hand down my side, lingering on my butt before he answers it. "Hello? Hey Fred. No, she's busy."

"Ask her how Granny's doing," I murmur into his chest.

"How's Granny?" he asks.

He rubs my back, listening to her talk and interjecting with, "Oh" and "That's nice".

Fred is living in Blue Falls and staying with Granny, at least for now. The day after Guy and Oliver appeared at Christmas, Granny fainted in the middle of an impromptu archery contest we were holding in the back-yard. Apparently, Granny had been having some "spells" but insisted it was nothing. When we wanted to take her to the doctor, she threatened to shoot all of us. Then, she bullied Fred into staying with her for a bit to mollify every-one, since Fred wasn't keen on coming back to New York, anyway. Fred has been giving us updates on Granny's condition, since she isn't one to admit to any kind of weakness.

I count out ten breaths before he says, "That's great, we'll call you back later, okay?" and then hangs up on her.

"I'm silencing your phone," he tells me, tossing it on the blanket behind him.

"Okay."

"What are you doing tomorrow?" The words are a rumble against my face.

Why is he asking? I could swear I already told him this morning.

I pull back and meet his eyes. "Catching up on work. I have to go sign the lease renewal on my apartment before the office closes at six, and I have to go through the list of trucks for next month and pick four of them to send to Oliver."

"What if you didn't?"

I wrinkle my nose. "I have to look them over. What if they totally stink? Oliver would kill me."

"No, I mean, what if you didn't renew your lease?" His eyes are dancing.

I frown at him. "Then I'd be a homeless wretch. Or I'd have to sleep in my truck which is not comfortable."

He laughs and ducks his head into my neck. "What if you actually understood my veiled references and moved in with me? With us?"

My heart stops in my chest and then takes off again at triple time. I sit up so quickly the blood rushes from my head. "Are you…really? Are you sure? What about—?"

"We want you to move in, too." Ava and Emma are both standing in front of us, holding hands. Emma pulls a necklace from around her head and hands it to me.

It's not a necklace, it's a key on a chain.

I take it from her with trembling fingers.

Ava nods solemnly. "We need a strong female role model."

I blink at all three of them, tears filling my eyes. "You mean it?"

Emma plops next to me on the blanket, tilting her head watching the tears fall. She frowns and pats me on the back. Then she pats the top of my head.

Guy chuckles. "Of course. I love you. I want you with me always. As much as I can have you."

"You're at our house almost every night, anyway," Ava says, rolling her eyes.

"I love you, too. All of you."

"Great," Ava says. "Now can we have ice cream?"

Guy laughs. "Yes, you monsters. You can get the money out of the front pocket of the picnic basket."

"Come on, Emma." Ava pulls at Emma, helping her to stand. "I'm sure they want to make out now."

Guy tugs me into his side and then rolls us both down on the blanket, tugging me into his side so we're lying face to face again.

"My lease ends next month," I say. "I would be living with you next month. You won't be able to get rid of me."

His smile is brighter than the spring sun dappling over us through the break in the trees. "Perfect."

Nerves flutter in my belly. What if I ruin everything? "But what if we live together and you decide you don't like something about me?"

He watches me, an adorable crease appearing between his brows. "Like what?"

I flap a hand. "I'm messy."

He shrugs. "I have a maid. And you're not that bad. I have teenagers."

"I have food stuck somewhere in my person, most of the time."

A flash of teeth at that one. "I'll enjoy trying to find it."

"But what if—?"

He leans over me, forcing me to my back, cutting into my space, an arm on either side of my torso. "What are you afraid of?"

I blink up at him. "Everything."

He runs his nose along my neck, sending shivers down my spine and straight to my lady bits.

"We'll have more opportunities to be alone if we share a bed," he says into my neck.

I breathe out a sigh. "Okay."

"Okay? That's it?" He pulls back to look down at me. "No more objections? Sex is what sways you?"

"What can I say? You know how to combat all my fears."

He laughs. "Remind me to scare you frequently."

And then we're kissing and I'm amazed all over again that all of my dreams are now my reality.

About the Author

Go here to sign up for the newsletter!
www.authormaryframe.com

Mary Frame is a full-time mother and wife with a full-time job. She has no idea how she manages to write novels except that it helps being a dedicated introvert. She doesn't enjoy writing about herself in third person, but she does enjoy reading, writing, dancing, and damaging the eardrums of her coworkers when she randomly decides to sing to them. She lives in Reno, Nevada, with her husband, two children, and a border collie named Stella.

She LOVES hearing from readers and will not only respond but likely begin stalking them while tossing out hearts and flowers and rainbows! If that doesn't creep you out, email her at:
maryframeauthor@gmail.com